Sniper

By Hilton Salomao Jr.

An amazing story of love and devotion

This book is dedicated to my wife for always supporting my dreams.

This book is also dedicated to all those elderly, regardless of being sick or not, who are abandoned in the streets or nursing homes, far away from their families, which don't lose their faith and hope. And last, but not least, this book is dedicated to pets all over the world that often suffer quietly and continue to love and revere their cruel owners, until their final days.

In memory of:

Giacomo Zuppo

In this book the author tries to express his repudiation of the abandonment of the elderly in nursing homes and the mistreatment and abandonment of animals.

This is a work of fiction in which the author tries to sensitize the reader, in a simple and objective manner, about the needs of the elderly and of animals, and also about how both are often dependent on the love and attention of others.

As it is a fictional book, the author doesn't intend to provide clarification about a diagnosis, types of treatment or surgical techniques.

Therefore, any likeness to the names of real people, places or events, is merely a coincidence.

Preface

This is the story of Sniper, the offspring of a golden retriever, an almost blind puppy that lived in a pet shop. His biggest dream was to have a family, but due to his vision problem nobody wanted him.

After a long wait, he was sold to a family, but his dream didn't last very long and he was returned to the pet shop.

Afraid and frustrated by the way he had been treated by the pet shop new owner, Sniper ran away but the city animal control caught him and locked him up.

Without family and abandoned due to his bad luck, Sniper had to work to survive. Quickly he was fired from all the jobs he had. After several attempts, Sniper was abandoned in Central Park.

Hungry, cold and afraid, our poor little puppy finally found a safe place to spend the night. That is where he met an old man, who was very good and caring. After a while Sniper discovered that this man, besides being very old, also suffered from Alzheimer's.

With love and devotion, Sniper will fight to save his dear master's life.

Hi, my name is Sniper and you must be wondering how I got here. So, I am going to tell you my whole story. Sit back, eat a treat and relax!

Chapter 1

This story starts in the pet shop where I was born. It was a very good place, everyone there liked me. Mr. Joseph was the owner, but to us he was like a father. I believed this because he always took very good care of us. He always fed us at the right time, it was really nice to always have good food and fresh water, and above all the place was very clean and organized, since Mr. Joseph was always cleaning everything.

There was only one thing that I didn't understand very well, it was the display window, because no matter how much he cleaned it, it was always foggy. This upset me because I could never see clearly what was happening outside of the shop. Children and their parents would always stop to play with me from behind the window. No matter what kind of cute puppy faces I made, they would turn and leave.

Like I said before, this was a pet shop and like any other pet shop, I didn't live alone. There were many animals there: birds, fish, snakes, cats, dogs, etc. My best friend was Jimmy, a German Shephard. Even though he was a puppy he was very strong and intelligent. We spent our days playing and pulling pranks. Mr. Joseph usually got upset with us when I broke something in the store, but it wasn't my fault, since he used to leave those objects in places that were difficult to see.

I always felt as if the shop was my own house, but despite this, I never felt very happy. My true wish was to be sold to real family, you know, with a father, mother, brothers and sisters. I always wanted to be part of a big family, but up until now that wish hadn't been fulfilled and maybe never will be. I was never going to give up hope, especially since I was a Golden Retriever and everyone tells me that I was cute and cuddly. Besides that, I was still just a puppy, so I had a lot of time.

Jimmy was older than me and was still living at the pet shop. He wasn't very worried about being sold to a family. The other day we were talking and he told me that his biggest dream was to be a police officer, also known as a K-9 in a dog world. I was sure that if his dream came true, he would become a great police officer.

The days at the pet shop were always the same. From behind the foggy display window it was impossible to see clearly, what it was like on the other side. I imagined it was a lot of fun, with all those people walking up and down, children playing and so on. One day I thought about running away, but I was afraid. I didn't know anything about the outside world and besides I was certain that Mr. Joseph would be very worried and upset. I knew that I was much loved, because a few days earlier, after having lunch, I took a nap and when I awoke Mr. Joseph was in front of me. Looking down at me, I observed that his eyes were full of tears. He had his hand on my head and he was stroking my eyebrows with his fingers. I thought that was very caring of him and the only reason for him to do that would be love. Since my health was outstanding, and I was very cute, cuddly and playful; perhaps that is why he liked me so much.

One Friday morning, Jimmy and I woke up and we saw that it was down pouring. Mr. Joseph served us our first meal of the day and after finishing our meal, instead of playing like we did every day, I laid down in the corner, looking out through the display window. I wasn't sick, but I felt a great sadness, somehow I knew that this particular rainy Friday was different. I knew that something very bad was going to happen. I was lying down for a good while until Jimmy came over and started licking me. Jimmy being my best friend was able to understand how and what I was feeling.

The day went by without any big news, I was already feeling a little bit better, the anguish I felt that morning had gone away some, but I was still feeling different.

It was almost six o'clock that evening, when Mr. Joseph was preparing to close the pet shop. Just then, two state police troopers entered, they were in uniform and they were very strong and tall. I noticed that Mr. Joseph stopped what he was doing to speak with them. After a short conversation, Mr. Joseph took the two policemen to his office. At that moment in time I knew that something was going on. Soon after, they left his office talking happily amongst themselves. I became very nervous and afraid when I saw the three men walking in our direction, but luckily the police officers changed direction and left the pet shop. Mr. Joseph continued doing what he was doing before and later he brought us our dinner and fresh water. Jimmy was also a little agitated, but he didn't say anything to me. Then Mr. Joseph said good night to us, turned out the lights and went home, closing the door behind him. Jimmy and I ate our dinner and because we were such good friends, we barely looked at each other. We both knew that something was different, but we were calm because that rainy Friday had come to an end and we were still together, safe and sound.

We slept well the entire night and we woke up very happy, we immediately started playing and running around the entire shop. Mr. Joseph came towards us and without saying anything, took Jimmy away from me. In the beginning I thought it was normal. I thought that perhaps Mr. Joseph was going to give him some medication, but after a few minutes the pet shop door opened, revealing the presence of the two police officers, the same ones that had been there the day before.

Within a few minutes I saw my friend being handed over to the police by Mr. Joseph. I got very nervous and I barked a lot, but it was all in vain, because I couldn't stop those two officers from leaving the shop, taking my best friend away. From behind that foggy shop window, with great difficulty I was able to see when Jimmy was placed into the back of the police car. In a few seconds the police car disappeared, just like magic.

I was just a puppy and after a few hours without my friend, feeling alone, I started to cry. Because I couldn't see clearly what was going on out there on the streets. The days passed, but things weren't the same without Jimmy. For me it seemed like all those days were the same, cloudy without any happiness, and because of this I no longer had the desire to play; I would just lie down all day, feeling hopeless.

After a few days, Mr. Joseph called the doctor, because, according to him, I was losing weight. My hair was falling out and all this for no apparent reason, because according to the doctor, I was in perfect health. Mr. Joseph must have become very worried, because he wasn't sure what was happening with me. He was constantly coming over to play with me and he was always bringing me new toys.

After a few days and with so much caring and dedication, I started to feel a little bit better. To me it seemed as if Mr. Joseph's love and protection was the best medicine. I don't know why, but in general, people with grey hair and wrinkled faces took good care and protected their animals and plants. Finally my weight went back to normal and my hair stopped falling out and it seemed as if I was even cuter than before, since I felt loved again.

One Saturday morning I woke up in a good mood and I was starving. I ran to have my breakfast and started to play, but I noticed suddenly that there

11

was something in the corner of the kennel. I was very curious and carefully approached it; it looked like a new toy. I ran toward it, but when I touched it I was totally shocked, because it wasn't a toy, but rather the newborn Labrador pup that Mr. Joseph had just bought.

After the shock wore off, I went to the other side of the kennel, apprehensive and confused. I started to think about my friend Jimmy; I remembered all the suffering and loneliness I felt when he was sold. I imagined that perhaps that newborn pup was also feeling very scared and was missing his mom a lot. After all he was over there without moving at all and shaking terribly.

Not wanting to scare him, I approached him carefully and started to stroke his tiny body with my tail. Because he was scared he didn't show any reaction. I thought that it would be better to lick the fur on his face. After licking his face, the puppy lifted his head and opened his tear filled eyes. I became very happy because I was certain that with the same caring, dedication and patience that Mr. Joseph had shown me, I would help him become happy again, just like Mr. Joseph had helped me.

Once again I was certain that I could help him, because within a few hours the pup seemed to be very happy. He didn't cry anymore and he was already even playing with some toys we had in the kennel. Little by little I realized we were becoming great friends, just like Jimmy and I used to be.

After a week, the puppy had changed; he was very clever and playful. He didn't seem anything like that frightened newborn. So I decided that it was time to give him a name and teach him how to pee like all the other male dogs, you know raising up the leg, since up until that point in time he had been peeing just like the female dogs.

I started to explain to him how to do it. How he should bring up his leg and which places were the proper ones, like posts, fences, etc. He paid a lot of attention to me, but when he lifted up his leg to pee, I was so shocked I almost died; he wasn't a boy, but rather a girl! The newborn puppy was a girl, my God how embarrassing. All that time I was peeing in front of her and talking about the female dogs that came to the pet shop to get groomed and bathed, boy I was very stupid. After all that, after that big scare, the only thing left to do was to give her a name, so I decided her name would be Daisy.

After my discovery, my relationship with Daisy was very different. I could no longer talk to her about anything and everything, nor could I play with her like I did before. I knew I had to be more careful, since she was a girl and as such deserved to be treated more gently by me, meaning no more rough housing. But just the same our friendship became stronger and more genuine, we started to sleep closer to each other and we would even share the same bone.

I always thought about my best friend Jimmy, I was worried about him and I was certain that he thought about me too.

One day when Mr. Joseph was cleaning our kennel, Daisy, who was very mischievous, grabbed a sheet of newspaper that was going to be used to line a part of the kennel. She started running around holding on to the sheet of newspaper in her mouth. Soon she tired herself out and dropped the sheet of newspaper near me.

I had one of the biggest surprises of my life when I saw a photograph on that sheet of newspaper, it was Jimmy. He was next to a police officer and he was receiving a medal. He seemed as if he was very happy about becoming a successful K-9, because that was his biggest dream.

It had been two months since Jimmy had been sold to the police and although I was very optimistic, I never gave up hope. I was getting worried, since up until that day I hadn't been sold. Maybe it was too late and maybe the worst is that perhaps I will never have a real family, one that would take care of me.

One sunny Saturday morning, Daisy and I woke up, had our breakfast and started to play next to the store window. We saw two kids looking at us attentively, and in a few minutes the pet shop door opened and those kids, accompanied by their father, came running in. They were very euphoric and happy. When I saw that man talking to Mr. Joseph, I started to cry. I knew they would take Daisy away, just like they did with Jimmy and I would be alone again.

After a few minutes of conversation, Mr. Joseph came over in our direction, looking happy and satisfied, and told Daisy and I that we had been sold to the same family. He would miss us a lot, but now we would have a real family.

Mr. Joseph prepared Daisy and I so that we could be turned over to our new owners. They seemed to be very good people, because they bought a lot of toys and leashes for us, all top of the line. The only thing they didn't buy was dog food; our new family was Italian and perhaps they would feed us imported dog food.

At last I felt that Mr. Joseph was overly satisfied. He knew that Daisy and I would keep each other company and that we would be very happy in our new home.

Chapter 2

Wow! When we left the pet shop I realized that our new family was bigger than I thought. There were six more men waiting outside for us. All of them were wearing suits and ties and they kissed Mr. Francesco's hands as he walked past them. One of them asked Mr. Francesco if we could get going. He opened the car door so that we could get in. The kids, Daisy and I all got in the car that looked more like a bus. It even had a small plasma television screen. For a few minutes the adults stayed outside by the car until Mr. Francesco and the driver finally got in.

The kids were very happy. Bruna, the youngest, was very loving. Right away she took Daisy in her lap and started kissing her. Vittorio on the other hand was the kid from hell. Besides not putting me in his lap, he threw me on the back seat. Finally, the car started moving and Mr. Francesco started listening to some very lively Italian music.

We arrived at the new house thirty minutes later. We all got out of the car and when Daisy and I saw the size of the yard we went crazy. We both started running around and playing. Everything there was very big. The house was enormous and very beautiful, but our happiness didn't last long. Vittorio, who was known as a little devil, grabbed the water hose and got us all wet. Bruna started to cry. Luckily one of the men that took care of the yard told Vittorio that if he didn't stop he would tell Mr. Francesco everything. Immediately Vittorio stopped. However, a few minutes later that same man told us we had to go inside the house.

That house really was truly big and there was a lot of space to play. I started running after Daisy, but I ran into a vase instead which fell to the ground and broke. I don't know why, but I swear that vase was farther away than it seemed to be. When the vase fell onto the floor, there was a loud noise of broken ceramic that could be heard from the rooms that surround the room I was in. Immediately, everyone ran into the room. Mr. Francesco became very irritated and upset and ordered me to be taken away. Bruna became very sad, but when I looked over at Vittorio he was smiling. Can you believe that they put me outside in one of those little dog houses? You know? The little red wooden ones. Luckily it was only for a few hours. I think that Bruna spoke to her father and he let me go back in the house.

It was already lunch time. After experiencing new things and playing so much, Daisy and I were starving. When they brought our food, we were very surprised because it was spaghetti Bolognese with meatballs. Daisy looked at me and we started laughing. I really didn't understand what was so funny since we always used to eat dog food. Then, I heard someone else laughing, it was Billy. He was a very old and fat cat. He was so white that he could be confused with a snow ball. After we saw him he came over to introduce himself and told us that in that house they always served Italian food.

I was very worried since this type of food is probably not healthy for us. Although I was worried, I devoured everything and it was extremely delicious. After lunch, Daisy, our new friend Billy and I were talking and Billy told us that everyone in that house was Italian, and they were very happy, but that they were part of an organized crime ring, you know, the Mafia. After all of Billy's explanations I was a little afraid, but I felt a little better when he told us that they all liked animals a lot. That is, with the exception of Vittorio who enjoyed mistreating everyone.

The days went by and sometimes I thought about Mr. Joseph. I remembered how he cared for all of the animals in the pet shop. I think he must have been all right, after all, only a week had gone by since we had been sold. Also, I sometimes remember the time when Daisy was just a puppy and how shocked I was when I found out she was a girl.

I have to confess something to you. Ever since Daisy was taken to the pet shop as a newborn we have had a very good relationship. But something had changed; I thought I was falling in love with her. After all, she had turned into a very beautiful and charming Labrador, aside from the fact that she was very dainty and was always worrying about me. One day when we went to have lunch, I almost ate the cat's food. I sincerely thought that Billy's plate and my plate looked a lot alike. Luckily Daisy pushed the plate away with her nose and stopped me from eating Billy's food.

We were all very happy because Christmas was coming soon. Daisy and I were very excited since that would be the first Christmas we would spend with a family. We were very anxious to receive our presents. One morning they started to put up the Christmas tree a few feet away from the dining room table, it was enormous with hundreds of decorations and colorful ornaments. Daisy, Billy and I were watching all the action and we really wanted to help, but we were just pets and they would only let us play with the empty boxes that were all around the room.

Daisy seemed to be very worried about me; she didn't let me get near the Christmas tree. I think she knew that something could happen. I listened to her and played far away from the tree even though all that shine from the ornaments and the decorations caught my attention and it appeared to be very difficult to keep my distance. Daisy knew me very well and knew that I wouldn't stay away from that Christmas tree for any length of time so she invited Billy and me to play in the yard.

When we got outside we started to play in the snow, it was very cold, but just the same we starting rolling over from one side to another. I was very curious and all of a sudden I saw something that was partially covered by the snow. Without losing any time, I uncovered a piece of rubber that I had bitten as I was trying to dig it out. I was shocked instantly by something that threw me backwards and made all my fur stand on end. It was an electrical cable and for the first time in my dog years I had been electrocuted.

Daisy and Billy ran to help me, but when they saw that I was fine they started to laugh a lot. I ended up laughing in light of the fact that I had a big scare, it was pretty funny.

We stayed outside a little longer until Mr. Francesco called us in. He had a funny Italian accent and when he spoke it was as if he was singing. We all went inside and I was very surprised when I saw a man with grey hair, I thought it was Mr. Joseph, but I was wrong. This man was Mr. Francesco's father, his name was Mr. Giovanni, and he came from Italy to spend Christmas with us.

He was a good man, as are all people with grey hair and wrinkled faces. It wasn't even Christmas yet and he brought me a gift. It wasn't anything special; it was just a long piece of wood for us to play fetch with. I ran towards him and grabbed my gift. Right away Mr. Giovanni fell to the ground. After all, it wasn't just any stick to play fetch with; rather it was the cane that he used to support himself. Mr. Francesco got very mad at me; he even yelled at me and ordered Vittorio to take me outside. Daisy tried to stop him since it was very cold outside, but she wasn't successful and in a few seconds I was outside behind a big glass door. The door was completely fogged up, but I was watching everything that was going on inside, even though it was difficult to see through the glass. It didn't take long for Daisy to realize that I was there and she came towards the glass door and lay down next to me. The large glass door still separated us, but just the same Daisy's presence warmed me up.

We spent the whole night there, until the morning when Bruna opened the door in her caring way, quickly called me to come inside. Within a few minutes she took me to the bathroom and gave me a warm bath. Regardless of everything, I was very happy because finally it was Christmas day.

After the bath, Bruna took me to the living room where everyone was waiting for us. It was time to open the presents. Daisy got a beautiful new outfit. Billy got a ball of yarn and I got a red ball that made squeaky sounds. Everything was wonderful; I didn't even remember what I had gone through the night before. We spent all morning there, playing with our new gifts until Vittorio; who never really liked us, started to play fetch, tossing my new ball so that I would fetch it.

It was getting close to the time to have Christmas lunch. Everyone was ready to sit at the table and Mr. Francesco told them to place Daisy's, Billy's and my plate on the floor near the table since, according to him, the whole family should celebrate Christmas lunch together. It was a magical moment. It was at that instant moment that I was sure that I really was part of a real family.

Everyone sat down at the table to have lunch, but before we started Mr. Francesco decided to offer a few words of thanks. I saw everyone lower their heads and closed their eyes, except for Vittorio who bent down to get my ball. I was very happy since we were going to play fetch again. I believed from that moment on Vittorio and I would be good friends. Daisy told me not to think about that, but at that time I wouldn't hold back and as soon as Vittorio threw my ball I ran after it. I don't know what happened, but when I went to fetch the ball I made that entire big Christmas tree fall on top of the table. It scared everyone because they heard the sounds of all the ornaments and decorations breaking on top of the serving platters and trays.

Everyone opened their eyes from the shock. Mr. Francesco, who got up and with his eyes full of anger, grabbed me and removed me from the dining room as he yelled at me, saying that I misbehaved one too many times and that this time there was no forgiveness. I hadn't only ruined the beautiful Christmas tree, but I had also ruined all the good food and the rest of the day. He added that from that moment on I would never enter that house again and that I was no longer a part of that their family.

After spending a while outside, a car arrived bringing many pizzas for everyone to eat. I was sure that this time Mr. Francesco got very mad because I spent the entire day and night outside.

When the morning came around, Bruna opened the door again and I was very happy since I was sure that my punishment was over. So I ran in her direction, but she kept crying and told me that there was nothing else she could do to help me. At that very moment I promised myself that I would try to be more careful. Mr. Francesco came outside with one of the bodyguards so right away I started doing tricks hoping that he would forgive me, but it didn't work, because he was still very angry. At the same time Daisy, who was crying a lot, ran in my direction because she knew what was going to happen. Before Daisy could get to me, the bodyguard grabbed me and put me in the backseat of his car. One of the windows wasn't completely closed which made it possible for me to hear Mr. Francesco telling the driver to take me back to the pet shop.

At that moment, images of all the happy times in that house passed before my eyes, as if it were a movie. Desperately, I tried in vain to get out of that car. In a matter of seconds it had started moving, leaving the home full of my wonderful dream of having a family and from Daisy, the love of my life.

Chapter 3

In spite of the sadness I felt for having been removed from that house and taken far away from Daisy, Billy and the entire family. I felt as if this wasn't a permanent thing. I felt that perhaps Mr. Francesco would change his mind and would send someone to get me at the pet store. I comforted myself by thinking that even though I was far away from everyone, I would have Mr. Joseph's love and care again. The trip back to the store was uneventful and as soon as we arrived, Mr. Francesco's bodyguard took me inside. Everything was very different. Aside from everything being out of place, there was a young woman working there.

I impatiently looked around in all directions trying to catch sight of my dear Mr. Joseph, who was certainly going to be happy to see me. After a conversation between the bodyguard and the young woman, I was taken to my old kennel again where the window was still foggy. I found a new guest there; it was Skip, an unfriendly and very dirty Rottweiler. I thought it was very strange that Skip would be in that condition; since I knew that no animal at that store had ever gotten to that point. I was certain it is because Mr. Joseph always cared for and gave a lot of love to his animals.

I tried to start up a conversation with Skip, but he didn't give me the time of day. He always avoided conversations and would growl non-stop. I became a little afraid at certain times when it seemed like Skip was going to attack me. I impatiently waited for lunchtime since I was certain that Mr. Joseph would bring our dog food and fresh water. As lunch time arrived, another man brought us our dog food. I had never seen anyone with such dirty clothes. His beard was long and instead of bringing two plates this man brought only one, which I tried to get close to. Skip was a lot bigger than me and he tried to attack me, showing me, I guess, that he was in charge now. I was really starving and I tried again to eat something, but was blocked by Skip. Then in an almost heroic fashion, I told Skip that whether he liked it or not, I had to eat and that when Mr. Joseph found out what was going on he would get angry at him.

For the first time that enormous dog showed a reaction, he looked me right in the eyes and immediately started to laugh uncontrollably. So I told Skip that there was nothing funny, I said that here everyone had always been treated with respect and love. Mr. Joseph wouldn't allow any of his animals to be treated like this.

Suddenly Skip's laughter stopped and he looked me right in the eyes and said that the old guy that I talked about so much was history, finished, in other words, Mr. Joseph had passed away. I felt like this was a distasteful joke since just a few weeks prior Daisy and I had left the store and Mr. Joseph was in excellent health. So, once again, Skip, now with a slightly more caring tone, asked me to sit down and he told me that a few days after Daisy and I were sold, Mr. Joseph had a problem with his heart. His daughter called the ambulance, but because of his age he didn't survive. Skip told me that after his death the store was sold and that it now had a new owner, one that didn't give a hoot about anyone. Skip explained to me that we would only get dog food once a day and that sometimes they forgot to bring us water. In addition, they never cleaned the kennel and this is why it was so dirty and unkempt.

I explained to Skip that it was inhumane, that even animals deserved good food and water, as well as a clean and organized environment. Skip laughed again and showed me a wound that never healed. He told me he felt a lot of pain, but that no one took care of him. He also told me that he used to be a happy, fun and a very loving dog until he arrived there. After seeing all the forms of mistreatment and abandonment, he lost hope for life. After our conversation, I became very sad, thinking of the wonderful memories I had, remembering the receptive environment that Mr. Joseph had always provided at that pet shop.

A few days passed and one morning after waking up I went to call Skip to go get our first meal of the day. He was still lying down, completely still, I thought that maybe he was very tired, aside from being a little old; he also had that wound that made him suffer and probably didn't allow him to sleep well. I approached him very carefully, not wanting to frighten him I only moved his paw. He didn't show any reaction, so with my head I tried unsuccessfully to wake him up, but he continued to stay still. After a few minutes I realized that something was very wrong since I did everything to wake him up and he stayed in that same position.

After a while, the young lady that worked as the store clerk entered the kennel to take away our plate when she realized that Skip was still sleeping. Upon trying to wake him, she discovered that Skip was dead. She called the new store owner who upon entering the kennel, simply pulled on Skip by his paw and without any love or compassion, complained only about the bad smell that the old carcass of that poor dog's suffering, emitted all over the inside of the kennel.

It was a very sad scene, but I was certain that Skip's suffering ended right there and that soon he would be up in the heaven together with Mr. Joseph, who I was certain would care for him with a lot of love.

Only one time did I think about running away from the pet store, but because of my love for Mr. Joseph I changed my mind. But now it was different, I knew that if I stayed there I would suffer a lot. Aside from the fact that several days had gone by and Mr. Francesco hadn't come to get me. So I was certain then that I had to do something to change my destiny, that I couldn't lose hope like Skip did. I had decided to write my own destiny. My name is Sniper and somehow I knew that I would have the opportunity to escape. I was determined and I knew that my mission couldn't end this way.

A few days went by, and one day when the pet shop clerk went to take the trash out, she placed a wedge by the door so that it would stay open. I couldn't lose that golden opportunity and before she realized it, I was good and far away from there.

Chapter 4

I walked for many hours after running away from the pet shop. I was very cold and I knew it was going to be a long night, but just the same I was happy and very hungry. While walking down a dark street, I smelled food, but I didn't know where to find it because it was so dark. Luckily a man opened a door which lit up the alleyway a bit, so that I could see that it was the back of a restaurant. The alley was filled with trash cans overflowing with leftover food. I hid in the shadows until the man finished smoking his cigarette and went back inside the restaurant, making it possible for me to finally get closer to those trash cans. I was very hungry and I knew that somehow I had to turn over one of those trash cans to get to the food.

Finally I was able to turn one of them over, one that was light and full of delicious food. It must have been put there a few minutes earlier because the food was still hot. After eating, I needed to find a place to sleep, it was already pretty late and I was very tired. Even though I wasn't comfortable, I slept well through the whole night; I think it was from the fatigue. In the morning I was awakened by the sound of the garbage truck coming to pick up the garbage, I left immediately, fearing I might be seen by somebody.

Another day was starting and due to the intense cold I knew it wasn't going to be an easy one.

I walked aimlessly for several hours until I came across a campfire underneath an overpass. I approached carefully, it was very scary and I was pretty frightened, but I had to find a way to warm up a little bit. When I was very close, I saw two people sitting near the flames, surely trying to get away from the cold as well. I stopped about ten feet away to determine how dangerous the situation was, but suddenly one of them called to me. Carefully I started moving closer when the other one threw me a piece of bread, which, without much thought, I ate quickly and moved away. Once again, they called me, this time a little more caringly. At this moment, I hesitated, but I got even closer and that is when I was able to see that it was a woman and child. The little girl came really close to me, kneeled down and started to play with me. I was very happy because I had found new friends.

This woman and her child didn't have anything, they barely had enough food for themselves, but they shared that little bit of food they had with me. I was very thirsty. This lovely lady placed a little bit of snow in a small pan and melted it over the flames of the campfire, quenching everyone's thirst. I'm not smart like human beings, but I would like to understand how it is that our government allows people to live in these conditions. At the same time they spend a ton of money building bombs that will only be used to kill other people. Well, just forget about it, I don't think anyone will ever understand it.

We spent the whole day by that fire, but when it started to get dark, the woman and her daughter got up and said goodbye. The woman said they had to go to the shelter and that there they didn't allow animals. I became a little bit sad, but I understood their motives, but alas, I was alone again. It was snowing again and those sweet people disappeared quickly because of the heavy snowfall.

I thought that this spot would be the best place for me to spend the night, so I got closer to the fire, which by now was a lot weaker. I couldn't do anything, because even though I wasn't a puppy anymore I was still just a kid. And even young dogs know that kids should never play with fire. As the snowstorm worsened the cold became unbearable and the strong winds were blowing a lot of snow underneath the overpass. Fortunately, I found a better place and I lay down to go to sleep. I fell asleep quickly, but I woke up soon after when I heard the sound of a truck parking. I thought that might be the garbage truck again, but before I couldn't even move; a man approached quickly and threw a leash around my neck. I had no chance to run away and every time I tried to wrestle loose; he tightened the leash around my neck. Within a few minutes he had put me inside the truck and to my surprise there were other dogs inside. I was frightened so I asked the dog closes to me what was happening, he told me that it was animal control and that we were being taken to a public animal shelter. Initially I was scared but then I thought about it a little and I calmed down. Well, that woman was also going to a shelter with her daughter and certainly she knew what was best for them.

The trip to the shelter didn't last very long. After a few minutes the truck came to a stop and the doors opened. We were all forced to get out of the truck quickly and we were all placed in a very large cage. The smell there was very bad and we all barked a lot. At that moment I felt bad for that mom and her daughter, perhaps the smell at their shelter was the same.

Soon they brought food and water for all of us. Of course it was nothing like the food we got at Mr. Joseph's pet shop, but at least it was eatable and we were out of the cold. As time went on, the dogs stopped barking, I think they barked because they were afraid, and thankfully after eating I was able to get a good night sleep.

Everything usually seems better in the morning, but not at this shelter. When I woke up I could see more clearly how dirty it was, I think if Mr. Joseph had been there, things would be different.

All the people that worked at the shelter treated us horribly, as if we were criminals. We were simply scared animals. For the most part they were all dogs just like me, who had most likely been abandoned by their owners. I couldn't stand that place, even though we had food and water, I preferred the company of the people I had met at the overpass.

I had already run away once from the pet shop because they mistreated the animals, and for certain I wouldn't be staying at that shelter for very long. Somehow I had to make an attempt to run away again. A few hours went by, and the employees started to separate us by breed, size and gender. When they got to me they went crazy, saying they had found gold. Of course everyone always found me to be cute and cuddly, but no one had ever compared me to gold.

After they found me there, they separated me from the others and started to treat me differently, more carefully, they even gave me a bath. After they separated me from the others they took me to my own cage that was very clean and neat. I also got a better meal than the one from the night before. Even with this special treatment, I wasn't completely happy. I found this discrimination based on my breed and appearance to be unfair to the other dogs.

After eating, I laid down to watch all the action. Just then a woman came in my direction. Her name was Mrs. April and she seemed to be concerned about the fate of all the animals. As she came closer, she opened my cage and told me I had visitors. My eyes filled with tears of joy, right away I started to imagine Mr. Francesco and little Bruna finally coming to get me. Once again I promised myself that I would try to be more careful and not break anything when I went back to their house.

With great difficulty Mrs. April pulled my up on her lap, after all I was no longer a puppy and she was about the same age as Mr. Joseph. I could tell because they both had grey hair and wrinkly faces. Right away she took me to another room where two police officers were waiting with their backs turned. To my surprise, when they turned around, I was able to see that they were the same men that bought Jimmy.

After turning me over to the police officers, Mrs. April smiled and said that maybe they could help me. The officers signed some papers, said goodbye to her and within a few minutes we were in the parking lot walking toward the police car.

Chapter 5

We were still far away from the police car, but just the same we were able to hear a soft, muffled barking. As we approached the police car, the barking gradually increased until we reached the car and one of the police officers opened the door so that we could get in. This was a definitive moment, I was certain that we couldn't get discouraged. There he was, Jimmy, my best friend, sitting still and staring at me. He was bigger, stronger but I was still certain that it was him the moment I saw him. Not just because of his scent, but because of the police dog appearance he had ever since he was a puppy. In the beginning he looked at me with doubt in his eyes. After all I had changed a lot, I was no longer a puppy and I had grown quite a bit since the time Jimmy had been sold off.

It didn't take long for Jimmy to recognize me too, perhaps because of my scent. The important thing to remember here is that we knew that our deep friendship remained intact even though we had been apart for some time. Perhaps it was even stronger now, given that we could confirm the fact that true friends never forget each other.

We started to talk about everything that happened after they separated us. Jimmy became very sad when he found out about Mr. Joseph's death. I told him everything that had happened to me and Jimmy made me feel better when he told me that from now on everything would be different, because I was going to be a K-9 too. Jimmy started telling me all about his adventures, including when he got a medal for bravery. I told him that I already knew about the medal because I had seen his photograph in the newspaper and that's what gave me a calm feeling when I thought about his destiny.

After all that talking and catching up on old times, we arrived at our destination, a training camp for K-9 dogs. Jimmy told me that everything he learned, and that it was a very good place. I was happy to hear this but also pretty worried, since I had never really thought about becoming a K-9. Besides as you have probably already noticed, I didn't see very well. The police officers opened the car door and I instantly got out and started running, so happy, waiting for Jimmy to follow me so we could play. But Jimmy called me back over and with an air of reproach, telling me that was a place of work and that there was no room for fun and games. I perceived that Jimmy really took this place seriously and perhaps that's the reason why he was so good at what he did. So, I decided to change my immature attitude, especially because I wasn't longer a young puppy.

The police officers took us to a room where they gave us a bath and soon after took us to a kennel that was full of German Shepherds, Labradors, Rottweilers and Golden Retrievers, all very well treated and well kempt. Jimmy told me to eat and rest because the following day, before my training started, the veterinarian was going to implant an electronic tracking device in my front paw.

I was terrified and asked him if this implant was going to hurt and what this electronic tracking device was for. He told me that the implant wouldn't hurt at all. The doctor would use a topical anesthetic on the area and after with a small incision, he would implant a GPS under the skin. He went on to say that the chip was smaller than a bean and that it was used for our own safety. For example, in case we got lost or were held prisoner someplace, the police could find us pretty quickly. Well, after these explanations and knowing that Jimmy was a great friend, I calmed down. Everyone ate their food in silence and then we all went to sleep. The silence was absolute. I detected that Jimmy wasn't the only K-9 that was very serious, they all were very serious. With so much silence, I fell asleep quickly.

I had a good night's sleep but, right before dawn I heard a very load siren. The siren was the signal for us to wake up and finally start the training. I was afraid and also very excited. I wouldn't only be having a surgical procedure but I also couldn't wait for the training to start. After all, this was my first job and I wanted to do everything just right!

It wasn't long before a nurse arrived and took me out of the kennel. In a few minutes we arrived at the clinical ward and the doctor started the procedure to implant the GPS. Jimmy was a great friend and he was right, it didn't hurt at all, and within a few minutes the doctor told me that was already capable to start my training. So, the nurse took me to an enormous field, where there were many machines, which made it look more like an amusement park, but in reality they were equipment to help us with our training. When I arrived I noticed the other canines were already there.

In a few minutes I would be starting the training and I was completely lost. I didn't know what I should do, so I asked Jimmy. He told me that there would be several different activities but that I would be the last one to do each exercise in order for me to have a chance to see them doing each of the tasks and then I would know in advance how to do them.

The first exercise was to go up some stairs and then after that, we would jump thru a flaming hoop. Everyone did this perfectly, but when it was my turn I tripped on the steps, everyone laughed, except Jimmy who just shook his head. I had to repeat the exercise but I fell again and this time it was down several steps. This was a really difficult task due to my very poor vision.

So we moved on to the second exercise. We had to apprehend a suspected motorcycle thief and after the police gave the order, I was supposed to attack him. I was sure this exercise was easy but when I received the order, I ran and bit the motorcycle tire. Everyone laughed again, but that time I didn't think it had been my fault, since the suspect was wearing rubber clothing. Very funny, what could I do since his leg looked like a motorcycle tire? I thought that everyone understood why I was confused, but when I looked over at the officer that gave me the order, I observed that he looked disappointed.

So, we moved on to the third exercise. We had to get out of the police car, run about ten feet, jump over a fence and then catch a fleeing suspect. Everyone did it so perfectly that it looked like a scene from an action movie. But when it was my turn, I got stuck on the fence, and it was so bad that they had to cut a piece of the fence to get me out. I thought that maybe because it was my first day of training that I had done very well. I was very proud of myself. Fortunately the training had come to an end and while we were waiting to be taken back to the kennel, I noticed that next to the police cars there was a wooden crate full of small metal balls. I was dying to play with one of those balls, and before anyone noticed I grabbed one and started running back and forth. When the police realized what was going on, they started to run after me like crazy. I was very happy because never had so many people wanted to play with me at the same time. One of the officers was able to reach me and he took the ball out of my mouth and threw it far from where we were. I did indeed try to get the ball, but he was holding me by my leash. On the one hand I was very sad when the ball exploded since that meant our game ended very quickly. On the other hand I was thankful that no one was hurt. In reality, that little ball was a grenade. How was I supposed to know that the marvelous little ball was so dangerous? After several officers arguing with me, they again took us to the kennel. Once again I was the brunt of all the jokes, not just because of the confusion during the training but also because of the episode with the grenade.

As soon as we arrived at the kennel, Jimmy approached me and asked me what had happened. He asked me if I had some vision problem. He also said that I should tell him the truth; after all he was my best friend. I was embarrassed and said that my vision was perfect, but that my vision was a little blurry that day. I asked him what was going to happen the next day and he said that we would be training on the streets, in a realistic setting.

During the rest of the day we stayed in the kennel and I had to put up with everyone's teasing until night time when we went to sleep. I knew that the following day would be special, since I would prove to everyone what I was capable of. Finally it was dawn and I hadn't slept the entire night. I had a lousy night's sleep because I was worried about the next day's training. We had a quick breakfast and then they took us to the parking lot where the police cars were. I was very nervous and I was afraid I was going to fail again, since I knew that I had a minor vision problem. I thought I could overcome this obstacle.

I asked Jimmy if we could go together and he told me that we couldn't. He explained that in each car there would be one police officer and one K-9. He also told me to be careful and wished me good luck.

In a few minutes one of the policemen came towards me and took me over to our vehicle. Even thought I was very insecure I was still very excited. Our car started moving and after a few minutes the officer received our assignment via the radio. They said we should head over to an abandoned warehouse because there was some suspicious activity happening at that location.

The police officer turned on the siren and we soon arrived at our destination. Very carefully and with his gun in hand, the policeman opened the door so I could get out; he took off my leash and told me to check to see if anything was going on inside the warehouse. I was feeling very useful and I knew that everything would turn out well. I cautiously entered the warehouse and started searching every inch of the place. When I pushed a door to one of the rooms, I caught sight of three men who were speaking in hushed tones. The room was a little dark but one of them turned around and I got a big surprise, it was Mr. Francesco, my former owner. He immediately remembered me. He bent down and called me caringly by name. I immediately ran over to him and we started to play. I was very happy, so much so that I thought he would take me back home with him. Mr. Francesco told me to lie down and be quiet. Then he got up and handed a white brick over to some other men who turned around and left from the other side of the warehouse. Mr. Francesco bent down again, picked up a stick that was on the ground and started to entice me to play. I always loved to play fetch. Mr.

Francesco threw the stick far away so that I would fetch it. I was ecstatic, so I ran and got the little stick but when I returned Mr. Francesco had disappeared. I looked for him for a few more minutes but found nothing. I decided to go back to the police car, still holding the stick in my mouth.

The officer was standing there waiting for me and from the look on his face, it was clear he was very angry. The office was very upset and yelling at me he said that I had let the criminals get away and that he was going to take me back to the base since I was a total failure. The whole ride back the police officer was still very upset but at least he had stopped yelling at me. Within a few minutes we were back at the base and the policeman took me out of the car and directed me back to the kennel. I knew that I had definitely disappointed him and that I shouldn't have played with Mr. Francesco but I missed him so much, I couldn't help myself. When I got to the kennel, there were no other K-9s there, since everyone was still working.

After a few hours Jimmy arrived, looking tired, but just the same he came and spoke with me. I told him everything that happened and he told me that he had already warned me that there wasn't a place for joking around. He also told me that he was very much my friend and he didn't want anything bad to happen to me. He added that perhaps this job wasn't ideal for me. Even without wanting to and feeling ashamed, I had to admit that he was right; after all. I knew that the job wasn't for me. Because after all, I was only a dog I had to do exactly what I was told.

Another day went by and out of respect for our friendship; Jimmy didn't tell the other K-9s what had happened. Even though deep down, I knew he was a little disappointed with me. It was already almost night time and everyone was getting ready to go to sleep when an officer came into the kennel and without a word took me out of there. None of the K-9s understood what was going on, with the exception of Jimmy and me. I was taken to an individual kennel to spend the night there. I didn't know what was going to happen in the morning and went to sleep thinking that maybe, the following day, they would take me to the doctor because of my vision problem. Or perhaps, they would give me more training. Either way, I was tired and I would have to wait to see what would happen the following day.

I didn't sleep well the whole night since I didn't know what would happen. Once again I heard the siren so that we would all wake up and in a few minutes, even though I was far away, I could hear the other K-9s barking. It was taking a long time for someone to come and take me out of the kennel so I started to worry about my destiny.

After a good long while, a police officer approached me, took me out of the kennel and told me that this work wasn't for everyone and that because of my efforts and my desire not to give up, that I deserved the opportunity to be happy and to have an owner who would care for me. Right after

that, he took me to the police car and in a few minutes
we were back at the public animal shelter, the one
that I had just left.

Chapter 6

When we arrived at the animal shelter, the officer opened the back door of the police car so that I could get out and very soon we were inside the building. Within a few minutes, I noticed that even though very little time had gone by, many things had changed. Everything looked cleaner and more organized. When Mrs. April saw us, she came over immediately, always smiling; she asked the officer how she could help us.

The office told Mrs. April everything that had happened and explained to her the reasons why he was bringing me back to the shelter. Mrs. April, who looked at me caringly, told the officer that she was very happy that I had come back and that she would do everything she could to find an owner that would love me for real. The officer thanked Mrs. April and told her that he admired her for her professionalism and dedication to the animals. Right away she thanked him for the compliment and the two said goodbye. That's when the officer left the room.

Mrs. April called one of the staff at the shelter to take me back to the kennel. Within a few minutes I was able to confirm that everything really was different, even though the animals were all separated by breed, size and gender, they all received excellent treatment. In addition to very high quality dog food and water, now everyone was treated with respect and caring, regardless of their appearance.

After I entered the kennel and started talking with the other animals, I found out the reason why there were so many changes. They told me that the new director at the shelter was Mrs. April and that since she took over everything had changed. They also told me that now we even had a veterinarian at our disposal and because of this, we no longer had sick animals in the kennel.

I was very happy after hearing all the news. Especially since I would now have the opportunity to have another family, since I knew that Mrs. April would keep her promise. After a while and after having already adapted to my new situation, we received our dinner, which was marvelous. After everyone had eaten, we started to talk about our experiences and that is what made me think of Daisy again. However, this time not just as a friend but as something more. My feelings for her now were different. Even with the distance, I loved her. I knew that this love was platonic, almost impossible, since I would probably never find her again.

After all the dogs had told their various experiences, we went to sleep since we were all very tired. The next morning I woke up very early, many of the others were still sleeping. I didn't have anything to do, so I sat down next to the kennel grille and observed the employees working. They did everything they could so that everything would be organized again that day.

Soon after that Mrs. April arrived and as always, without delay she came to the kennel to see if everything was in perfect order. She insisted on entering the kennel to play with each of the animals. She knew that this loving gesture was very good for all of us. When it was my turn, on top of playing with me, Mrs. April told me that she had made an appointment for me to see the veterinarian. She wanted him to make sure that I was in perfect health and perhaps he would give me some vaccines and more importantly, do an eye exam. Remember, the police officer that brought me back there told Mrs. April that there was something wrong with my eyes. He told her that when I was training to be a K-9 that I got stuck in the fence and also fell many times during the exercises.

So, the appointment with the vet was already set, so the only thing left for me to do was to wait anxiously for this important meeting. Somehow I always knew that I had a vision problem, especially that one time in the pet shop when I woke up and saw Mr. Joseph crying while he was patting my eyebrows. I was afraid of this consult because I knew that there was a problem with my eyes. It could be something serious and that horrified me. Time was passing and my anxiety was growinge even more. The truth is, even thought I was afraid I couldn't stand waiting any longer. I wanted that nightmare to be over as soon as possible.

To pass the time more quickly, I thought it would be better to play a little with some of my new friends. But before I even realized, Mrs. April approached the kennel and with the help of the nurses took me out of there. Then they took me over to the much awaited consult. I was going to be seen in one of the rooms at the shelter that had been set up with several medical devices. The veterinarian was waiting for us impatiently. When I saw him I was terrified, but because of his experience and love of animals I quickly calmed down. First I had a clinical exam, and then right afterwards they gave me some vaccines that I needed. I noticed that veterinarian was very young, almost a kid, but despite this he knew what he was doing. All of his movements where made caringly and carefully. Yet even with all that care I still felt very apprehensive, since I still didn't know what was wrong with my eyes.

When the clinical exam was over, the vet told Mrs. April that my health was very good and he asked that the nurse take me to the other room where my eye exam would take place. A few minutes later I was transferred to the location where, once again, I would be examined by that kindly doctor.

The veterinarian started the procedures necessary to carry out the exams. Mrs. April was there right by my side and also tried to calm me down by patting my shaking body. After several exams and tests, the veterinarian revealed to Mrs. April that I was suffereing from hereditary cataracts. When I heard these words I was totally horrified. I thought that my end was in sight, but when the veterinarian explained to Mrs. April that this disease affected canines early on, especially Golden Retrievers, and that this little problem could be treated with a simple surgical procedure, I felt much better. After all, I wasn't going to die because of this and perhaps, after the surgery I would start to see properly.

After the veterinarian's explanations, Mrs. April sat down and told him that it would be impossible to carry out any surgery procedures, because the amount of donations to the shelter had gone down and that they didn't have enough money, not even to keep the shelter open for much longer. At that moment I became very, very worried about the shelter's financial problems, not because of my surgery, after all I had that problem for a long time and I had learned to live with it. But I was particularly worried about the animals' future in the event that the shelter was to close down.

Well the consult with the doctor was over and finally I was much calmer, since my problem didn't seem to be so serious. However our shelter's financial problems made me think of that woman and her daughter that I had met under the overpass. Maybe the shelter where they spend the night was also having this kind of problem and if it were to close, that sweet woman and her little girl wouldn't have any place to sleep.

So, as soon as the consult ended I was taken back to the kennel where all my friends were waiting for me. They were all anxious since they knew that I was afraid of the diagnosis. I was very hungry when I came back from the consult, but before I could eat I had to explain to everyone what had happened. Of course I didn't tell them about the shelter's financial problems. If I did, everyone would become very worried ahead of time and for no reason. After all I knew that Mrs. April was going to think of some way to solve this problem. I also knew that the people that always made donations to the shelter would help again and that the problem would be solved.

After explain to everyone how the consult went, I ran over to my plate where my dog food was waiting. It was so delicious that when I stopped for a minute I realized I had eaten everything. That was a very tense day for me and so right after my meal I went to sleep.

I had a magical night; I dreamt about Mr. Joseph, Daisy, Jimmy and even that nuisance Vittorio. But most of all I dreamt about the possibility of a new owner. The next day I woke up very happy, it seemed as if the problems and discoveries from the day before had been nothing more than a nightmare. When we got our breakfast, I was certain that the shelter was in dire straits because what they served us wasn't enough for everyone.

We were all good friends and we ate what each of us needed. So each dog ate only the essential amount so that there would be enough dog food for everyone. We had our breakfast and after a few hours, Mrs. April came over in my direction saying that she had found a new owner for me. She opened the kennel for me and with the help of one of the staff she got me out of there. That was so unexpected that it seemed to be part of the dream I had the night before. But it was reality, it was happening and even thought it was a surprise I was quite happy because my dream was once again turning into a reality.

They took me to the bathing and grooming room so that they could get me ready to meet my new owner. While they were giving me a bath, Mrs. April mentioned to her employee that the shelter could close at any moment and that she would have to give all of us away. It was especially difficult in my case since they omitted some things when they told Mr. Ronald, my new owner, about me, like my vision problem. Aside from doing that, they also told him that I had been trained for certain jobs, which was obviously a lie since I had, up until that time, only been trained to be a K-9 and even that had been a total failure. When I heard this commentary, I was very intrigued but I knew that everyone there respected and liked all of the animals and for that reason I knew that they wouldn't doing anything that would make us suffer.

As soon as they finished, they took me out of that room and quickly took me to Mrs. April's office where Mr. Ronald was waiting for me. But when she opened the door, I realized that he was blind. I was very happy and proud but then my big surprise came when she told him that I was going to be his new guide dog. When I heard that crazy statement I started to laugh. This could only be a joke. But when I realized that she was being serious, I laid down and played dead. Right after that Mr. Ronald called me over to pat me caringly, but when I went over to him, he started patting my bottom. Mrs. April and I thought that was very strange. Suddenly he started to laugh and apologized telling us that he thought he was patting my head.

I admired Mrs. April very much but this time, I thought she had gone crazy. Imagine with my eye problems, with my sight being so bad, I could easily be considered legally blind. As a K-9 I had caused so many problems, can you imagine this now? This was going to be a true disaster.

Chapter 7

Mr. Ronald was very happy and quite pleased after signing all of the adoption papers. He got up from his chair and asked Mrs. April to help him put my leash and guide gear on me. He was very familiar with the equipment, but with Mrs. April's assistance he was able to put it on me faster. So within a few minutes I was ready to start my new job.

In spite of my limitations, I decided that somehow I would help Mr. Ronald, even though this task was almost impossible, since literally I would have to be his eyes and guide him wherever he went. Mrs. April said goodbye and kindly walked us to the door. This time she wished me good luck. After leaving the shelter, I felt that this job wasn't going to be easy. Mr. Ronald thought I had been trained to do this job, unfortunately I was just a dog and I couldn't warn him about the truth. Well, at least I would try to do anything I could to guide him safely.

My first mission was to take him to the nearest bus stop so that we could go to the supermarket. Everything seemed to be going well, until, we arrived close to the corner where there was a phone booth. I was able to maneuver around the booth just fine, but it wasn't enough, Mr. Ronald bang his head into de phone booth. When I heard the sound, I turned around and saw that the poor guy was dizzy. So for a few minutes we waited right there, long enough for

Mr. Ronald to go back to normal, mainly getting back his balance, since he was pretty shaken up.

We stayed there for a few more minutes until he decided to move on. I definitely wanted to stay there a little longer, perhaps forever, but at least until we wouldn't run into any more danger. But I had no choice and we started up again on our course, heading toward the bus stop. Luckily we arrived at the corner and were able to cross the street safely. However, when we arrived to the other side, Mr. Ronald tripped badly on the curb, so badly that I thought he had ripped out a piece of the concrete! He screamed so loudly that everyone who was nearby ran over to try to help him.

I knew that I should have warned him, but I didn't notice that the curb wasn't the kind for handicapped people. Poor thing, that time I really thought that he felt a lot of pain because his eyes filled up with tears. Mr. Ronald had a lot of spunk so a few minutes later he wanted to keep going as if nothing had happened. It's a good thing he couldn't see, because certainly he would cry if he saw what the tip of his shoe looked like. We had to get to the supermarket so we continued on in the direction of the bus stop.

Even though I could barely see anything, I continued to guide Mr. Ronald, like I good guide dog would do. Thank God nothing else happened. I finally was able to see the bus stop. I was very happy to have guided Mr. Ronald there without any more injures. After a few minutes the bus that we were waiting for arrived. The bus driver already knew Mr. Ronald so, even though we didn't flag him down, he stopped and opened the doors and waited for us to get on. You know I have never really liked stairs, since they always seem to blur my vision.

The bus driver was very patient and waited for us to have the courage to get on the bus. However, Mr. Ronald appeared to be very anxious, I think that perhaps he knew what was going to happen. I mustered up the courage and started to head up the huge steps. Mr. Ronald was right behind me, holding the leash so that I could lead him inside the bus. But when I was almost at the top, I tripped on the last step. This time it was even worse because I dragged Mr. Ronald with me all the way down the steps. We were lucky because the steps weren't as big as I thought, so after falling we didn't even have a scratch on us. Mr. Ronald became very upset since he had fallen on top of a stack of trash bags and from the smell of them it seems they had been there for some time. They did however serve as a buffer which avoided him getting hurt.

At this point, the driver and a few other passengers came to help and get us into the bus, which was jam-packed. The smell of the trash had infiltrated Mr. Ronald's clothes and within a few seconds spread throughout the bus. I noticed that everyone tried to ignore us and move as far away as possible. The smell was really very strong, so much so that even I was having trouble breathing. Luckily the supermarket wasn't very far from where we were, which meant we would arrive at our destination shortly. A few more minutes passed by and then the bus driver gave us a heads up so that we could get ready since our stop was the next one. We quickly got up and waited anxiously for the driver to stop and open the doors.

Finally, we arrived at our destination, but as I was going down the steps I didn't see that the bus driver had stopped the bus on top of a big puddle of water. So, unfortunately, once again, I caused us both to step into the almost frozen water. You can definitely be certain that I cannot serve as a guide dog, since some kind of incident happens at every turn of a corner. And regardless of how calm he was, I knew that these incidents were making him very mad and regretting his decision to adopt me.

Finally we were able to get to the supermarket and we started to do the shopping. Everything was fine and he seemed to calm down a little bit. Then, all of a sudden I ran into a pile of glass jars filled with tomato sauce and everything came crashing down around us. I think this time I went too far, the damage was pretty bad. Many glass jars broke spreading tomato sauce everywhere. Quickly the supermarket employees came over to see what had happened. Mr. Ronald was so upset that he sat down and started to cry out of anger.

When I saw him sitting down like that, I started to laugh. He looked like a meatball on top of a plate of Spaghetti alla Bolognese! A few people helped him get up and he decided that he wouldn't do the shopping any more. Before I realized it we were already heading back to the street. I was also tired from so many problems. I started to imagine how many other incidents would occur until we got to his house. Then, for the first time ever, this guy had a good idea and we took a taxicab and luckily the taxi driver didn't have any vision problems. So, in a few minutes we arrived at his house.

I was very hungry, since it had been a while since I had eaten. And on top of that, after so many adventures, I was feeling pretty tired. Soon after getting home, Mr. Ronald gave me dog food and fresh water. I ate quickly and went to sleep since the following day I knew I would have a lot of work to do.

I slept well that night, but right after I woke up I decided that I should stop trying to be a guide dog, since I was putting our lives at risk. Somehow I needed to let him know this, but since I was only a dog I didn't knew what to do. A few minutes went by and then he came over and quickly got me ready for another day of work. He put on my leash and other gear, all the necessary equipment for a guide dog to do a good job. Unfortunately I needed a lot more than that; I needed a lot of good luck.

After having experienced so many problems the day before I couldn't understand how Mr. Ronald still trusted me. Nonetheless, within a few minutes I was already ready for work and heading to the street where our destination that day would be Mr. Ronald's office which wasn't very far away. Thank

God he decided to walk up to the office and to my luck, stay away from public transportation.

He lived in Manhattan and therefore, even though it was a short distance, it meant we could encounter dangerous situations. We would have to cross a few streets, and you all know that for people who are "perfect" this is already dangerous, so imagine what it is like for handicapped people, especially the visually impaired. In other words, it could be fatal and I knew this very well…

It didn't take long for us to arrive at the first intersection. It was a super busy one, but luckily for us, there were a lot of people waiting for the light to change. When the light changed all I needed to do was to follow the people that were there until we got safely to the other side. I was feeling pretty confident since I thought that this is what would happen at all of the other intersections.

I had a lot of confidence in myself at this moment and I think that Mr. Ronald did too, especially since up until that time nothing had gone wrong. We still had a few more blocks to go before we arrived at our destination and even feeling more confident I knew that many things could go wrong, after all I didn't see very well, actually I was almost blind too!

We were approaching another street corner and I noticed that we were close to the intersection of Broadway and Times Square. I knew that it was a very dangerous intersection and that we would need lady luck to be on our side to reach the other side.

Especially since it was a long way to cross over to the other side, and not to mention that many streets crossed through here. Just the same I was happy because I knew that Central Park was close by. I knew this because I could already detect that peculiar smell of the horses that worked over there.

We finally got to the corner and luckily there were many people waiting for the green light so that they could cross the street. I had to think quickly and I decided that, like the previous intersection, we would follow them again. But, when the light turned green, everyone went in different directions and I got confused and didn't know which way to go. Since I had to cross, I started moving forward, but when I was almost in the middle of the intersection I heard a lot of people yelling, cars honking and in addition to other noises that I had never heard before, several cars had crashed, some were on top of others. It was horrible. Within a few seconds, someone came to help and get us out of there.

When we reached the other side, the people there told Mr. Ronald that everything had been my fault. They told him that the accident happened because a bus that was trying to avoid running over us braked abruptly causing a huge pile-up. Mr. Ronald wanted to stay there a few minutes longer to be certain that everyone involved in the accident was all right. Luckily, despite everything that happened, no one got hurt. I was very frightened by everything that happened, but something inside me told me that an incident of this nature couldn't have been avoided.

I thought that Mr. Ronald was going to keep going, but all of a sudden, he bent over, took off the leash and the harness that I was wearing and he told me that he couldn't take all these problems anymore. Within a few seconds, he got up and entered the first taxicab that appeared. He left me there, without knowing what to do. Everything happened so quickly and it didn't take long for me to realize that I had been abandoned again. A few minutes later, I recovered from all that and was actually feeling happy since I wouldn't have to do something that I knew was doomed from the start.

I was alone again and my dream of having a family was over. I had lost hope but as unhappy as I was, I had to find a way to keep going, to try to find a reason to live. There was nothing else I could do, I had to keep living. So, I decided to go to Central Park, because I figured I could find food there and mainly, I would find kids there that would want to play with me.

Chapter 8

After walking for few blocks, I finally arrived at Central Park. I was tired and very hungry too, but luckily it was a wonderful day and the park was full of children. Regardless of the cold and the few snowflakes that still covered the grass, the kids came over to play with me right way. I was very lucky; some of them even offered me something to eat.

I was having a lot of fun with all of that, but after a few hours, the children started to leave, one by one, taking with them the few and brief moments of happiness that I had that day. I knew that the following day other children would come and that I would have company again, but this would always be a passing thing, like the clouds that come and go. Before I even noticed, all of them had gone home and the sun went down, but I decide to stay there for a little while longer, after all, I didn't have anywhere to go.

I always thought that Central Park was a very beautiful and fun place, but when night came, I was terrified. That wonderful place became deserted and scary. After the sun completely disappeared, the temperature started to drop, it was already night time and I had to find a sheltered place to spend the night, because if I stayed there, I would certainly die from the cold, so even though I was very scared, I decided to look for a place and I ended up going deep inside the park.

I walked for a few minutes, until I discovered a spot underneath a small bridge, the place was frightening, but it was sufficiently safe for me to be able to spend the night.

I was very tired and I lay down near a column, I was exhausted and I fell asleep before I even realized it. I slept well the entire night, but when I woke up, I noticed that there were some newspaper sheets on top of me. I got up as quickly as I could and I saw that there was a man sleeping a few steps away from me. He was also covered with newspaper and it wasn't difficult for me assume that the man had covered me up and that's why I had been able to sleep well the whole night without feeling cold.

After realizing that I wasn't alone, I returned to the spot where I had been sleeping and I waited there for him to wake up. Even though I was feeling apprehensive I wasn't afraid of him, after all, he was concerned enough to cover me with the newspaper while I was sleeping.

It seemed like he was very tired since he had been there a long time and he wasn't even moving. That scene reminded me of what happened to Skip, so I decided to get closer and somehow discover whether or not he was ok. So, when I pulled back one of the newspaper sheets that were covering him, I had a pleasant surprise. He opened his eyes and smiled at me. Besides, his face was all wrinkly and his hair was totally white.

At that very same moment, I started to lick his face, letting him know how grateful and appreciative

I was for what he had done the night before. He was very surprised by my presence, as if I had just gotten there. Nonetheless, I had found myself a new friend, who reminded me quite a bit of Mr. Joseph, but my heart told me that there was something different about him, something very special.

After we played for a few minutes, he told me his name was Robert and that he would be my new owner; I was very happy about that, since I thought I would never belong to anyone else. This definitely filled my hearth with happiness.

We had already been awake for a while, but up until that point in time, we hadn't had anything to eat. Although I was happy, I was very hungry and I thought my owner was too. Luckily I think he knew what I was thinking and he grabbed a bag with a few pieces of bread in it, just enough for our breakfast.

I knew that he didn't have anything else besides those few pieces of bread and the torn clothes he wore. So, I decided that when it was lunch time that I would go out and get us something. After all, we were still in Central Park and since there were so many people, mostly tourists, it wouldn't be difficult to find something to eat. Besides, somehow I had to pay him back for all that he had done for me.

Well, after breakfast my master called me over to him. I obeyed right away, after all, he was like family now and that was the only thing that really mattered to me. When I moved over close to him, he put me on his lap and very lovingly patted my fur. With all that caring, I felt like I was the only family that he had too. At that moment, I decided that even with my vision problem, I would do everything I could to make him happy and help him with whatever I could possibly do.

Lunch time was approaching, so I got out of his lap and as I had planned, I went out in search of something for us to eat. I was hard for me to leave him; since I was afraid I might lose sight of him and not be able to find him again. After all, he didn't know what my plan was since I was just a dog and cannot communicate with him using words!

Even though I was apprehensive and afraid, I left my dear owner and I went, where I knew I could find food. As soon as I got there, I checked out a few people and slowly I started getting closer. Then I started to play with the kids, because this way I thought it would be better to get someone's attention; someone who might give me some food. I was totally wrong. The clock was ticking and I didn't have anything, not even a breadcrumb!

I wasn't sure exactly how long I stayed there, but I was felt horrible for Mr. Robert, because he most likely very hungry. Besides, he might be worried about my disappearance. I was almost at the point of giving up, when a couple came over and one of them tossed two sandwiches to me. They were hot and inside a paper bag.

Quickly I grabbed the bag with the sandwiches and I got out of there as quickly as I could, literally running in poor Mr. Robert's direction. I figured that he was probably waiting for me and that he hadn't had anything to eat until then.

As I was running in his direction, that is where my new owner and I had been that morning, I couldn't stop thinking about what would happen if I went the wrong way back and got lost. Fortunately, a few minutes later I arrived at the exact same location where we had been and I spotted him. He was washing his face in a pond and while I waited for him to finish I watched the poor old guy more closely and realized that he was already quite old and that perhaps because he didn't have a house or any family, he was quite disheveled and unkempt.

The clothes he wore were very old and dirty, in addition to being torn. On the other hand, they appeared to be of good quality and also very expensive. They actually were a lot like the clothes Mr. Francesco used to wear. However, I knew that Mr. Robert could never buy such expensive clothes, in other words, probably someone had given him those clothes. The one thing that was for sure was that those were the only clothes he owned.

After a few minutes my owner finished what he was doing and came over in my direction. I automatically let go of the paper bag that I was still holding onto with my teeth, but when he got closer I was totally caught off guard. Instead of being happy for me being back, he simply asked me if I was lost and where my owner was. I was really perplexed about his attitude, because just a few hours earlier he had told me that he was my new owner, shared the few pieces of bread he had so we could had breakfast together and he acted caringly toward me.

At first his attitude seemed really strange to me, but I was certain that it was just a joke; after all, he couldn't have forgotten about me that quickly, right? So, I pushed the paper bag with the sandwiches in it over to him using my snout so that finally, my dear Mr. Robert could finally have lunch.

Slowly and with some difficult, taking into account his advanced age and his overall weakness which was most likely caused by the lack of food and having been abandoned, my owner bent down and picked up the bag with the sandwiches. He then shared the food with me again which made me very happy, since I was starving at that point. While we devoured our sandwiches, my owner stopped for a moment and informed me that as soon as we finished eating he would help me find my owner.

I was eating, but when I heard his words, I was dumbfounded. I also stopped eating because at that point I was certain that my owner wasn't kidding, he definitely didn't remembered me. For a few seconds I doubted myself; after all, I was almost blind and I could have confused Mr. Robert for someone else. My sense of smell was however, spectacular and even in the dark I could find just about anything.

When we finished eating lunch, Mr. Robert kept his promise. A few minutes later we were already walking around, according to him, to find my owner. I knew that this search was in vain; after all, he was my new owner, but for some reason he had forgotten this fact. When we were walking in the park, we came across some pretty strange people, one of whom upset my owner to the point he got very nervous and somewhat out of control. It was a woman who was going for a walk. She had her two kids with her and they were strapped around the waist with leashes, as if they were dogs. Mr. Robert told her that what she was doing was absurd, that should be considered a crime, since leashes should only be used on animals that posed some kind of danger to someone.

My owner's knowledge and rationale moved me and everyone around us. However, that woman was more concerned about holding onto her cell phone than about the comfort and dignity of her children. In other words, it didn't change anything; she went on her merry way as if nothing had happened. After walking around in vain for some time, searching for my supposed owner, who in reality was by my side the whole time, Mr. Robert gave up and said that we could continue looking the next day.

I was very happy about his decision to stop that stupid search, because I was totally exhausted and I think he was too. I could hardly wait for us to go back under that little bridge, where we had slept the night before. But once again I was surprised at his forgetfulness. He told me that we should go back to his mansion, where he thinks we spent the last night.

This poor man definitely had some kind of problem with his memory. I wasn't sure what it was, but I had to find out quickly, so that I could avoid going crazy on top of being blind. At this point I was already getting used to him and I had to go with him wherever he went, so that I could protect him from himself.

I knew that his problem made him a prisoner in his own body. However, I was tired of walking and for a moment I was happy that he forgot things fast. After leaving Central Park, right away we stopped under a marquee and he said that we had arrived at the place where we had spent the past few nights. It was already getting dark and we were tired and hungry. My dear master lay down, leaning against the wall and held me close to him. Luckily, winter was coming to an end and the temperature was a little higher than the night before. Just the same, we still felt a little cold, so I stayed nice and close to Mr. Robert's body.

I laid there for a long time waiting to fall asleep. While I waited, I watched the passersby as they went by the marquee. Some were in a hurry while others were moving slowly. This somehow made me think of my own life and of all those who had been a part of it. I mainly thought about Mr. Joseph's friends who always went to the pet shop, sometimes to chat, sometimes to buy something for their pets. When I thought about these times I remembered of a Mr. Joseph's friend who would always go to the store to talk to him. Their conversations always started out happy but then this friend of his would start crying, saying that his wife was getting worse every day. According to him there was no cure for her problem and that often times she couldn't remember what she had said or done and that lately she barely remembered him, her own children and even her own name. But what shocked me was when I found out that she had even forgotten how to hold a fork to feed herself.

During one of these conversations I was able to overhear Mr. Joseph tell his dear friend that Alzheimer's was a very ungrateful disease. It usually affects people of 65 years old or older, but sometimes it can affect people as young as 40 years old, and it really doesn't have a cure, but with love, caring, attention and understanding; people with Alzheimer's can have a better quality of life. He also said that one of the biggest concerns of the family members was to not let the Alzheimer's patient go out unaccompanied since they would definitely not be able to get back on their own.

After remembering all these facts, I finally realized that I had discovered what was happening with Mr. Robert. All of the symptoms he showed made me certain that he wasn't crazy, but that he was suffering from Alzheimer's disease and that probably he had gotten lost and couldn't come back home on his own. That is if he really even had a house.

I felt really sorry for Mr. Robert. I knew that the next morning he would wake up and he wouldn't remember anything, not even me. But I was determined to help him and I decided that I wouldn't leave him alone again because I would definitely lose sight of him.

The next morning we woke up and as I had guessed, he didn't remember me and again he was surprised that I was there, but I wasn't worried since now I realized what was happening.

I knew that my beloved master was suffering from Alzheimer's and I also knew that I should try to get him some professional help, the sooner the better, since according to Mr. Joseph's friend, this disease evolves.

Well, this was a huge responsibility for me, perhaps bigger than all the rest, and even with my vision problem, I had to find a way to help him.

A few days went by and no matter what I thought of, I couldn't come up with a way to help him. Partly this was due to the fact that this is a silent disease and there are no obvious physical side effects. In other words, no one would really notice that my dear owner was sick and needing help.

Chapter 9

Due to Mr. Robert's illness, I couldn't leave him along during the day, not even for a few minutes. So, I decided that I would go out to look for food at night while he was sleeping. I knew it was going to be very difficult to find someone who would give me something to eat, but I didn't have any other option.

For many nights, I went out in search of food and luckily New York is a very big city, so I was always able to find something. But it wasn't always enough; sometimes I didn't eat so that he could eat. After all, what little I could get, I gave to him since he needed it more than I did.

The weeks went by and each morning my master seemed to be weaker and sicker. I didn't know what else to do. The fear took over me. Even though I was an optimist, I couldn't find a solution. The despair and anguish I felt from seeing my dear Mr. Robert get worse and worse each day started to take a toll on me. But I had to remain calm and hopeful. Even though I knew that the food I got every night wasn't sufficient, I couldn't get discouraged. Especially because Mr. Robert didn't only need food, he also needed medications and these would be impossible to get without the help of a human being.

It was already spring time and as you know, it rains a lot at this time of the year. One night after going out to look for some food, I was caught by surprise by a bad storm. I had to seek cover and found some shelter under the marquee of a large supermarket.

Even at night time the supermarket lights lit up the whole area. These lights allowed me to see a sign that was hanging up on one of the walls. I was always very curious and when I got closer I could see that it was a poster with the photographs of people who had gone missing. Miraculously one of the photos was of Mr. Robert, who was next to a younger woman and a very beautiful Labrador who was wearing a pink ribbon around her neck. Mr. Robert's face stood out in this photo, leaving no room for doubt about his disappearance. Seeing that photograph brought a mix of emotions that overwhelmed me at that moment. At that very moment I had discovered that my master had a family that loved him and for some reason he had gotten lost and couldn't get back home because of his disease.

I remained under that marquee for a long time, waiting for the storm to pass. That night I wasn't able to find anything for my master to have for breakfast, but just the same I went back happy just to be with him. After my discovery I knew that we would make substantial progress, after all, I knew that his family was also looking for him and perhaps with my help, they would find him. The desperation and anxiety that I had been feeling turned into courage and determination. These feelings made me feel strong again and the hope of seeing my dear Mr. Robert being loved and cared by his family made me believe in me once again.

One more time we slept really close to each other, the early morning cold kept trying to take the place of the beautiful and colorful flowers of spring. But it was all in vain because every day new flowers blossomed, bringing with them a sense of hope for the new day. I kept going out every night looking for food. Every once in a while I would even go to the supermarket, so I could admire Mr. Robert's photograph on that sign. This always made me feel hopeful again.

One night when I got there I discovered that someone had taken down the poster with his photograph. In its place they put another poster, also of disappeared humans, but this time they were of children of varying ages. This surprised me on a profound level, since I couldn't understand how these most likely healthy kids could have disappeared. Nonetheless, I had enough problems of my own and even though I became very sad when I found out that millions of kids had disappeared, I couldn't do anything about it.

I think that the big companies could change this situation, showing photos of these kids in their commercials, associating their products with something so important. This way they wouldn't just be bringing profits to the company but also the respect of the entire population. Well, I was just a dog, but I still think that the high level executives of the big companies are smarter than I was, or at least they should be. When the poster that had Mr. Robert's photo on it was replaced I was very sad for several minutes, but then this sadness turned into happiness, since many kids would also have the opportunity to be found and be returned to their families, so that they could be happy again.

The days passed and we were already in full-fledged springtime. All the flowers had bloomed and there was a constant warm breeze. Even Mr. Robert seemed to be doing better, but I wasn't sure if it was because the days and nights were warmer or if it was because he was getting more food, but the fact of the matter was that he looked better and his mood was better.

One fine Sunday we woke up as usual, but this day was different than all the others. My loving master hadn't forgotten who I was, like he normally did every morning. For the first time ever he remembered me. He was very loving toward me and after having our breakfast; Mr. Robert got up and said we were going for a walk in Central Park. I was beaming and as much as I tried I couldn't remember anything in my whole life that made me feel so happy. I was certain that even though I was blind I had made a difference in that poor man's life.

We walked around Central Park all day and regardless of his illness, my owner was a fun old guy and very loving and caring toward others. So, it wasn't hard for him to get the guy that sells sandwiches at the park to give us two hot dogs. We were very hungry, so we sat down right there to have lunch. While we were eating, the sandwich guy spoke to Mr. Robert about a lot of topics including the international financial crisis of 2008 and the unemployment crisis it caused. They also spoke about how it left traces of uncertainties in many countries, mainly the U.S.A., where millions of people lost their homes and their jobs. I noticed that Mr. Robert's eyes filled with tears, but luckily for him, my poor old guy would forget everything, not because he was inhuman or unjust, but because of his illness.

After their conversation ended, my master got up, thanked him for the wisdom-filled sandwiches and wished him good luck. It was getting late so Mr. Robert decided to go back to the marquee where we had been sleeping for a while now. The sun was about to set making the Central Park look even more beautiful than ever. That amazing day had come to an end and I knew that my owner's improvement was a passing thing and that probably he wouldn't remember anything the next day.

We continued walking and in a few minutes we arrived at our old marquee. We were very tired, but I knew that the night was coming and with it came my responsibility for getting us food, like I did every night.

It wasn't nighttime yet, but Mr. Robert was very tired and after lying down he fell asleep very quickly. This rarely happened because of all of the noise from the cars passing by; the people that walked close to us and also because of all of the lights. Just the same, I couldn't afford to lose any time since quite a few stores and restaurants were still open.

Also, there were a lot of people still out on the streets which made it easier for me to get our next meal.

In a matter of minutes I was already walking on the streets looking for food, actually I was about to get to the restaurant when I saw a woman, who looked a lot like the woman in the photo that I had seen on the disappeared people poster. She was leaving a pet store, at first I didn't give it much thought, but when the driver opened the door so that she could get in, a Labrador, also identical to the one in the photo, ran out of the store and jumped into the limousine.

When I saw the Labrador leaving the pet store, I was certain that they were the ones from the poster, in other words, I had finally found Mr. Robert's family. Instinctively I started to bark and ran toward the limousine, which started to leave before I got to it. I was a few feet away from the limousine, barking like crazy, when the Labrador stuck her head out the window and started barking too. My legs went weak when I heard the unmistakable sound of her bark, because I knew with all certainty that it was Daisy. Simply put, the love of my life that I hadn't seen since the day Mr. Francesco ordered his men to take me back to Mr. Joseph's pet shop.

All that emotion lasted just a few seconds, because a young and beautiful woman, probably Mr. Robert's daughter, closed the limousine window before they took off. Just like in a dream, the limousine started speeding up and in a few moments it was gone, lost among all the cars and trucks. But this wasn't a dream, it was real and now, more than ever, I had to find my master's family, which the love of my life was part as well.

I stayed still for several minutes to try to regain my strength. As I was waiting, I was thinking about how Daisy ended up where she was, that is, what happened to her? Perhaps Mr. Francesco's family had also abandoned her. After regaining my strength and coming back to reality, I went on about my business. After all, my main objective was to get food for our next meal and take it to our shelter under the old marquee.

I walked for a few more minutes until I got to the back door of a restaurant. I found a bunch of barrels with leftovers in them. I quickly took what I could before someone saw me and went back to our shelter.

I was very tired so after putting away our food in a clean spot and out of the reach of any bugs, I laid down next to Mr. Robert, who was peacefully asleep. Even thought I was very tired, it took a while for me to fall asleep, because I kept thinking about a plan to find out where my owner's house was and how to get him back there.

I didn't even realize when I started to fall asleep. I was so tired that I had a very deep sleep, but when I woke up my dear owner had disappeared and the few belongings he had were strewn all over the place as if someone, for some reason, were looking for something. I got up suddenly and didn't know what to do. My heart was pounding so quickly that I thought I was going to have a heart attack at any moment. So I decided that I had to calm down before I did anything else.

As you know, when we are upset about something the best thing to do is to breathe deeply for a few minutes until we regain total control. And that is exactly what I did until I felt calmer again. Well, after a few minutes I was already feeling much better, so I decided that the first thing to do would be to look for Mr. Robert. After all, he could be lost and needing my help.

When I decided to go out to look for my dear owner, he showed up out of nowhere bringing with him an old broom and saying that our living room was quite dirty and that we needed to clean it quickly before the guests arrived.

My dear owner's disappearance left me quite upset, but this time the sadness and anxiety that I felt when I witnessed his deliriums was even worse, so much so that it made me cry. The day before he seemed like he had improved a great deal, but unfortunately this was just temporary. Well, the important thing was that we were back together again, safe and sound. This is what brought me a sense of great interior peace.

After we finished cleaning our little castle, I ran and brought the food I found the night before to my adorable master. Although it wasn't much, just a few pieces of chicken and three pieces of bread, we did have something to eat for breakfast and that was a good thing because we were both very hungry.

Chapter 10

After all those turbulent events that morning, I started thinking...how could I find Mr. Robert's family and take him back to his home. I knew this would be one of the most difficult tasks of my life and I also knew that it was crucial since that poor man urgently needed to receive love and care from his family. More so, he really needed medical attention and medication, at least something that could slow down his disease's progression.

Once again, I took a deep breath searching for answers, which effectively helped me find solutions. One thought that came to mind was what if every day I went back to the pet shop, where by chance I came across the love of my life and probably my master's daughter too. Maybe this would create a chance to see them again. After all, Daisy looked very beautiful in the poster of missing persons, but she was even more beautiful in the flesh. One important thing I noticed was that both times that I saw her, she had the same kind of bow around her beautiful neck. Maybe it was even a multicolored bow, but I can't confirm that since all of us canines are colorblind, so we cannot distinguish one color from another.

Well, I already had a clue and I knew where I needed to start my search but first I needed a plan. Especially, because I couldn't leave Mr. Robert alone during the day since most certainly he would leave the marquee and would get lost. On the other hand, I needed to keep watch at the pet shop every day in the hopes that the woman who I suspected to be my master's daughter appeared, hopefully bringing along the love of my life to get a shot or to just get groomed.

The fact is that as much as I would think about it, I couldn't come up with a solution. Of course I thought about asking him to go with me to the pet shop, but this notion was absurd, mostly because I wouldn't be able to communicate with him using words.

I didn't fear that any physical harm would come to my dear owner, after all we were in Manhattan, the heart of New York, and it is considered one of the safest places in the world after the September 11th, 2001 terrorist attacks. In fact, my only concern was to not let him alone, because for sure he would get lost due to his illness. Taking into consideration how big New York City is, it would be very difficult for me to find him again.

In a desperate attempt to find a solution, I went so far as to wish that Mr. Robert were a K-9. At least that way he would have a GPS in his paw, making it easier to find him no matter where he went. At that moment, without even realizing it, I had an idea that within a few minutes became more and more concrete and real. At first I thought I was going crazy, but the only solution would be to take out the chip that was under my skin and somehow hide in under my master's clothes in a place that not even he could get to. Otherwise he could find it and throw it away or even lose it, which wasn't hard to do considering it was a tiny little chip.

Well, the only way I could get the chip out of my front paw was making a small incision and taking it out with my mouth. But I couldn't do this during the daytime because my dear owner would certainly stop me from doing so. Even though he was sick, he still did everything he could to protect me, and certainly he wouldn't allow me to do such a crazy thing!

I decided to wait until the evening so that right after Mr. Robert fell asleep, I could start the procedure. I was determined to do it, even though I knew it would hurt a lot. But in this case, any pain was worth feeling since I had to save a life, the life of the man that I loved so much.

It was already night time and I was determined to do it, but the truth is that I had always been a fearful dog. I always was afraid of the dark, of strangers and mainly of feeling pain. Even when I had to get vaccines, I would get so scared but this time I had to confront my fear and moving forward with my plan.

After dinner we played for a few minutes until he lay down and said good night. He was very tired and within minutes he was snoring. It was finally time to start the procedure so I went to the other side of the marquee, as far away from him as possible so that I wouldn't wake him up in case I made any noise.

I lay down and when I went to start the little procedure I realized that I didn't have any instruments, so I decided to bit my own leg in an attempt to break the skin and remove the chip. I couldn't put this off any longer because if I did, I knew I would give up so I bit my leg and I bit it without holding back, finally cutting my skin in the exact spot where the chip was located.

It was very painful, but immediately I felt the chip between my teeth and that made me very happy since I was finally able to get it out and because the cut was superficial, it barely bled at all. The only thing left to do was to hide the chip in one of my dear owner's items of clothing. After thinking about it, I decided to hide it under the insole of the shoe he always wore and that I knew he would remove just when he went to sleep.

Everything was all set so that I could put my plan into action in order to find my dear master's daughter again and Daisy too. But since it was still night time, I had to go out again to find some food for us.

Even though the cut on my leg had been superficial, it still hurt a lot but just the same, I went out in search of food. I limped along for several blocks until I found something. Then I went back to the marquee and went to sleep. After all I needed to rest a little bit before starting out on my new adventure as a detective. It was early morning when I went to sleep and I knew that I would have just a few hours of sleep before the sun came up. However, I was very tired and even though it was just for a few hours, I slept soundly.

I think I overslept because when I woke up Mr. Robert was already having his breakfast. So, I quickly got up and went to eat something, but because my dear owner is very perceptive, he noticed the cut on my front leg. He was always very kind to me and caring, so right away he grabbed a bottle of water and a small piece of soap and cleaned out my wound. According to him, that little cut could get infected if I didn't take care of it.

I wasn't sure how, but my master had a small first aid box, so right after he cleaned the wound he disinfected it and put a bandage over it in the hopes that it would always stay clean and avoid becoming infected.

The first few hours of the morning had already gone by and I was still in the same spot. I knew that the pet shop would be opening soon and that I needed to get going since the place was several blocks from us and I needed to be on the look as soon as the store opened. After having breakfast I said good bye to my dear owner, licking his wrinkled face and before he knew it, I was already far away. The whole time I was running to the store I was worried about him since most likely he would think that I had abandoned him.

Even though Mr. Robert took good care of my wound, it was still very fresh and it hurt a lot when I ran. But my desire to get to the store was bigger than the pain and within a few minutes I was already in front of what I consider paradise, that place where all the animals wanted to be. Well, I was right in front of the pet shop, but I really needed to find a place to hide quickly because if I stayed there for very long, someone might call the animal control department. If that happened and I they caught me I would have to go back to that public animal shelter, kissing good bye to all hopes of finding Mr. Robert's family.

For a long time I looked for a safe place to hide, but I wasn't having much luck. Most likely there were no places near the store that could serve as a hideout with the exception of the popcorn stand. So, I thought that might be the best place for my hideout since the strawman might not mind if I stayed there if we became friends. Then I really wouldn't have to hide since passersby would think that he was my owner and no one would call the animal control department.

I got closer to the popcorn guy and after doing a few tricks he totally fell in love with me. I even went so far as to think that he too wanted to be my owner, but luckily I already had my own Mr. Robert and I didn't want to push my luck. Imagine if he wanted to take me home with him, if this happened I would be dead meat. Well, after made the popcorn guy fall in love with me, I received a bag of popcorn, freshly popped popcorn. So, I quickly scooted under the cart and stayed there eating my popcorn. But mainly I was attentively watching over the pet shop.

Chapter 11

After I lay down underneath the popcorn cart, I started to watch over the pet shop, which had just opened. I knew that the day was going to be long and tiring, after all, I was going to stay there all day long. I knew it was going to be boring, but there was nothing else I could do except to wait. Perhaps I would get lucky and Mr. Robert's daughter would bring Daisy on the first day. This would be a long shot since luck rarely is on my side!

It was still pretty early but the pet shop customer's had started to arrive and most of them were accompanied by their little pets. It was very nice to see all of those pets being treated well by their owners. After all I was one too, but while I was watching I couldn't stop thinking about the enormous number of animals that had been abandoned by their owners. They are now stuck living in public animal shelters, in uncomfortable quarters and without any love and attention. But I really got emotional when I thought of the millions of children around the world that for one reason or another were abandoned or had lost their parents under tragic circumstances.

If it is difficult for a pet to live without its master's love, imagine how difficult it must be for the millions of little children living without their parents' love.

Well, it's really up to the governments around the world to create incentives for adoption since this would be a great way to solve that part of the problem.

The hours passed and there was no sign of Mr. Robert's daughter. However that was my first day there and certainly I was prepared to continue coming day after day until she appeared. I stayed under that popcorn cart the entire day; I was very hungry since I had only eaten a bag of popcorn in the morning. Luckily night was approaching and as soon as the store closed, I could return to my owner.

As soon as the store closed, I got out from under the popcorn cart and I returned as quickly as I could to the marquee. Aside from being worried I also was missing Mr. Robert a lot. Thankfully when I got back, I found my dear owner there.

As soon as I saw him I was happy, after all he hadn't gotten lost and he seemed to be doing well. But as I approached where he was, I realized that he had forgotten who I was again.

When I left in the morning, I knew this might happen since my dear old friend was sick. But I didn't get discouraged and I started to play with him as usual. Luckily after a few minutes he gave in to my charming gestures and we became friends again.

I was hungry and very tired but just the same I started to get ready to go out in search of food like I did every night. When, all of a sudden, my master threw a big piece of ham over to me. After eating the ham, I played a little bit more with my dear owner and I went to sleep. I knew that the next morning I would return to the pet shop.

Two weeks went by and I kept going to the store every day, but nothing happened. I was already losing any hope of finding Mr. Robert's daughter and the love of my life. Once again, I was discouraged and down mainly because my dear owner was getting worse...he had even forgotten how to button up the buttons on his own shirt and that was making me feel hopeless.

One fine morning after saying goodbye to my lovely old man, I stopped in front of the pet shop as always and even after having lost all hope, I laid down again under the old popcorn cart. The wait, after so many days, had become monotonous and tiring but luckily the popcorn guy loved me to death so he bent down again and gave me a bag of popcorn to eat. Instinctively I pulled the bag close to me, but before I could start eating it, I saw Mr. Robert's daughter's limousine park in front of the pet shop. Finally!

I was so happy when I saw Daisy get out of the limousine that my legs were paralyzed for a few seconds. Right away I regained my strength and ran in her direction. As I was running I started to bark like crazy, which got everyone's attention, including hers. She turned around and when she saw me she started running in my direction.

When Daisy finally got to me we sniffed each other and Daisy surprised me with a kiss. Unfortunately, all that barking and running around also caught the attention of the limo driver who quickly ran over to get Daisy.

I couldn't let the driver take her back, because I would definitely not have another opportunity any time soon to see her, so I told her that we needed to run away from there as quickly as possible. Even though she had no idea what I was talking about Daisy agreed and before the driver could reach us, we were long gone.

After a few minutes we were already far away from everyone, mainly the driver who by that time had already called Mr. Robert's daughter to let her know what happened. After running like crazy for a few minutes, I was already feeling pretty safe so I told her we could stop running, after all I couldn't stand it anymore and I think she felt the same way.

As soon as we stopped running, I invited my true love to drink some water from a little fountain close to where we were. She immediately accepted my invitation mainly because she was also very thirsty. We walked for a few minutes to get to the fountain which was in Central Park, very close to the place where I spent my first night and where I also met Mr. Robert, my dear owner.

After drinking a lot of water, we moved away from the fountain and I was finally able to take her to the place where I started to find happiness. When we got to the little bridge I told her that this was probably one of the most special places that I had ever been. She started laughing and told me that perhaps I should look for a veterinarian so I could be examined since I was most likely going crazy. According to her, we had been to many places that were much better than this one, much more comfortable. Daisy was always right, that place really wasn't very comfortable, to tell you the truth, it was awful. So, then I told her that place for me wasn't special because of the comfort it gave me, but rather because of the experience I lived through there.

When I told her this, Daisy stopped laughing immediately intrigued and curious, she asked me what kind of experience someone could have in that place that would be so special. So, I kindly asked her to sit next to me and then I started to explain everything to her. I told her everything that had happened including how I met my new owner and everything about his illness.

Daisy listened attentively, to everything I said, but suddenly she interrupted me and told me that her owner's father also suffered the same problem, but that sadly he had disappeared a long time ago. She also told me that her owner, Mrs. Thelma, had already done everything she could to find him. Then I asked Daisy how it was that her owner's father had gotten lost. She told me that one morning the governess of the house where they live left the house with him and that after a few hours she came back and was very upset and told Mrs. Thelma that her father had disappeared. Daisy also told me that as soon as Mrs. Thelma found out that her father went missing, she called the police to file a missing person's report. She hired several private investigators and even placed ads on missing people's bulletins, but unfortunately to no avail, Mrs. Thelma never even received a phone call that would give her a clue about her father's whereabouts.

After listening to her give me all the facts I started to cry, not out of sadness, but out of happiness. Not only I knew where her owner's father was, but I also loved him very much. I now knew that all of my efforts weren't in vain and I was about to tell her everything. Even though she knew how emotional I was, Daisy didn't understand why I was crying. So in a mix of emotion, gratitude and happiness and with tears still falling, I told her that I had found her owner's father and I also told her that the place that we had been earlier was so special for me because it is exact place where I met my new owner, dear Mr. Robert, which was also her owner's father.

At that moment, two tears came to her beautiful eyes and ran down her face, certainly, these were emotional tears of joy. Seeing her so fragile, I ran my front paw over her face, lovingly and instinctively Daisy came closer and kissed me. For a few seconds we looked straight into each other's eyes and without saying anything, we knew that something very strong existed between the two of us. Somehow we knew that we were in love, but more than that, we knew that we truly loved each other.

After so much news and emotions, I knew that we needed to pull ourselves together. Even though our hearts were young and healthy, they should go back to beating normally. To help us calm back and also to find out why she was living with Mrs. Thelma, I asked her what had happened. I really wanted to know if Mr. Francesco had also abandoned her. She told me that Mr. Francesco had gone to prison and that he was going to stay there for a very long time. All of his pets were taken to the public animal shelters.

Daisy told me that she stayed at the shelter for a few weeks until Mrs. Thelma went to the shelter and adopted her. Worried and curious, I asked Daisy what had happened to little Bruna and with that pesky Vittorio. She told me that Bruna was living in a temporary adoptive home, waiting for a family to adopt her and that Vittorio was doing time in a juvenile facility.

I was very sad when I learned what had happened to little Bruna. She didn't deserve to go through all that, after all she was a good little girl, loving with everyone. Even though I didn't like Vittorio, I was curious to find out what he had done to be sent to a juvenile prison. So, I asked Daisy what Vittorio had done, what was so bad to have made him be sent to a juvenile prison. She told me that he was convicted of mistreating pets and trafficking wild animals.

Well, after Daisy clarified everything about her and the others, she wanted to know if my vision had improved or if I kept seeing blurry. I told her that I had Hereditary Cataracts, which it was a simple illness and it could be treated with a simple surgical procedure. Then I revealed to Daisy that even though this was a simple illness in terms of treatment that it was progressive and that is why my case was so complicated since I had already lost all sight in my left eye and the right eye was pretty bad too, because I could only see shapes. So, out of pity and caring she came close and kissed each of my yes and told me that Mrs. Thelma could help me.

I really wasn't very worried about my vision problem, after all I was born with it and I was used to it. So, I told her that my priority was to help my dear owner, Mr. Robert, since he suffered from Alzheimer's disease, a progressive disease, without cure. Again I told the love of my life that we urgently needed to take my master back to his house so that Mrs. Thelma, his dear daughter, could take him to the hospital and start his treatment as quickly as possible. Since my dear owner was very weak, he would certainly not live for very long without medical attention.

Daisy was frightened when I explained to her the seriousness of my owner's problem. She immediately wanted to go find him to finally help him, but it was already very late and I suggested to Daisy that we spent the night there, taking into consideration the dangers at night and the fear that we would be caught by animal control again.

Daisy agreed with my suggestion, after all we needed to rest since the next day we would have a lot of problems to solve. So we lay down very close to each other and while we waited for feel sleepy we went back to the way things were when we were little pups and we lived in our dear Mr. Joseph's pet shop. Daisy thanked me for all of the caring and protection that I gave her the day we met. It was getting very late and after talking for a long time, we became sleepy and without even realizing it, we fell asleep.

Chapter 12

We slept through the night and were unexpectedly awoken by the sun's rays which had already started to warm our bodies. Daisy woke up startled, since she didn't want to lose any time. I told her it was still very early and added that probably my dear Mr. Robert, was still sleeping and that we had sufficient time to get our breakfast and then calmly, go meet up with my poor master. After all, the marquee where he was sleeping was very close to where we were.

Daisy and I went out looking for something to eat for breakfast. After eating we got up and went in the direction of the old marquee, where our adorable old man spent his nights and a good part of the day too. We walked for a few minutes and Daisy was carrying a plastic bag in her mouth. It had a few pieces of bread and a donut that we found in the trash can at a dinner near Central Park. We wanted to take something better to him, to help relieve our loveable owner's hunger, but unfortunately we were only animals and that was the best food we could get for his breakfast. Finally we arrived at the old marquee that barely protected that very fragile man. He was flimsy not only due to his age, but also because of his terrible disease that made him suffer in silence. As far as he was concerned, everything was fine. He had no idea how bad his health was and what was wrong with him.

As we approached the marquee, Daisy and I both saw Mr. Robert's body all covered in newspapers. For a moment I was afraid to get any closer, not because I feared his reaction, but rather because perhaps we had arrived too late. I feared I may have lost him forever, without even having a chance to save him. After all this poor man was the only human being that really loved me, even though he was sick he found the strength inside to show me his love and caring.

Daisy knew me very well and right away saw my apprehension. She knew better than anyone else that the poor man that was there was probably the most important thing in my life. So in the hopes of ending my suffering, Daisy walked over toward my owner and after a few steps she finally removed the newspapers that were covering him up.

After Daisy removed the newspapers that were keeping poor Mr. Robert warm, a sense of indescribable tranquility overcame me and filled my heart. My dear old man got up and to our surprise; he called me over to him. Daisy mouth dropped to the ground, she was so surprised, since she could never have imagined that someone with Alzheimer's could remember their pet so easily, mainly because our friendship was so recent and it was difficult for my adorable master to remember me or my name. This is why I was really certain that my love and dedication to him were somehow helping him to overcome one

95

of the main symptoms of the disease, which was forgetting recent facts and information. Finally I ran over to him and I must admit that I felt a little jealous when I saw Daisy sitting on his lap. But it was right that she should be there, after all, in some ways she also belonged to him.

We played there for some time, sticking close to our lovable owner. There were moments when everything seemed totally normal, but unfortunately, it was a false sense of normalcy because the problem was still there and there was no stopping it. Daisy and I needed to find someone who could help us. We knew that the best way to get help was to take Mr. Robert back to his home, so that his family could help him. But how could we do that, in other words, how could we make an old and frail person follow two dogs for many, many miles until we arrived at our destination? So, Daisy and I had no other option, but to leave him there and make the trip back without him.

After thinking about all this for a few minutes, I called Daisy over and I explained my plan to her. Immediately she was against it because it was a risky plan. We risked never finding Mr. Robert again if he left that location. I explained to her that I had already thought of that a long time ago and that I had hidden a GPS under the sole of his shoe. Daisy looked at me like she didn't understand a word I was saying. After all, she didn't even know what a GPS was, so I explained to her that when they were training me to be a K-9, they had implanted this electronic device under my skin and that the device was used to locate the K-9 police dogs. So, if they got stuck somewhere or if there was an emergency, they could be found. So then she asked me how was it that this device was now under the sole of our dear owner's shoe if it had been implanted under my skin.

I told her that out of love and an act of desperation, I had bitten my own leg and removed the chip. After my explanation, Daisy remained in silence for a few minutes and then all of a sudden she hugged me with her eyes filled with tears. I gave my love, a few minutes to regain her composure then I asked her why all the tears. She told me that my love and dedication to my dear old man was something truly moving.

After a fraction of a second, I told her that my dear owner was the only human that had really loved me and that certainly he would do the same for me if I needed him to. Besides Mr. Robert was already old and sick, so I had to love him intensely for as long as he was alive. He definitely wouldn't be around forever.

After all of these explanations, Daisy was more confident and less worried now, because she knew that if our owner got lost we could find him again with the GPS's efficacy. But something was still bothering her and since I have always been curious, I asked her what she was thinking about. Then Daisy explained to me that it wouldn't be enough for us to simply arrive at our dear owner's house, but that we had to take something with us that would prove to

Mrs. Thelma that her father was alive and that we knew where she could find him. As I listened to her talk, I immediately remember the missing people's poster that I had seen on the wall at that supermarket. Since it had been something that made an impression on me I didn't forget the details of that photo. Almost instinctively I grabbed the old hat that my owner used and showed it to Daisy. I told her that certainly Mrs. Thelma would recognize that old hat as soon as she saw it, since it was the same one that Mr. Robert used before he disappeared. Daisy agreed with me immediately, because she also remembered not only the hat but also other details from the photo I mentioned earlier. At last our problems were finally solved. The only thing left to do was to start our long journey back. Since this would be a long and dangerous trip if we did it during the night, Daisy and I, although we were anxious to get going, decided to start our journey the following morning. So, now we had a few more hours to play with our owner.

The rest of the day went by without any big news and when it was night time Daisy and I went out looking for food. We knew we had to get enough for everyone, so that made us take a little longer. After getting what we needed, we went back to the marquee, we all ate and then went to bed. Daisy and I were both really anxious and we didn't have a good night's sleep, we were tossing and turning all night.

We really had a rough night, but luckily the first birds to awake started to sing, announcing the start of a new day. This was a day I had waited for during a long period of time. It was definitely going to be exhausting, but decisive as well for all of us. Right after hearing the birds sing, Daisy and I got up, said goodbye to Mr. Robert, grabbed the old hat and took off. That is when our long waited journey began...

It was still very early and the first few rays of sunshine were still hiding in the shadows of dawn. There were only a few vehicles on the streets of Manhattan; the majority of them were trucks and small cargo vans that made deliveries every morning throughout this region. Since it was early, there were very few people on the streets, most of them very young. They were leaving nightclubs and bars, some of them sober, some of them drunk. In the future they would regret that they spent so many nights out on the streets instead of spending them at home with their family and loved ones.

Daisy and I walked for a long time, until we started to see the first newspaper and magazine stands turn on their lights to start another day of work. I couldn't stand holding the old hat in my mouth, mainly because, as you know, dogs sweat through their tongues, so the hat was already slobbered over and it felt like it weighed a ton! I couldn't take it anymore, so I stopped and asked Daisy to stop too. When I explained to her the reason for stopping she simply laughed and said that perhaps I also had cataracts in my brain, since according to her, the place for a hat was on one's head. So as a gesture of solidarity, but still laughing a lot, she took the hat from my mouth and put it on my head. She was right; our head was made for thinking. For a moment I felt really stupid, but since I was a dog I knew that I would soon forgive myself.

After a few minutes, we started walking again. The first rays of sunshine had already broken through the Manhattan sky. Luckily for me, they would dry off the old hat more quickly. The number of cars and people on the streets and avenues had already increased considerably, so it wasn't difficult to conclude that another work day in one of the most populated cities in the world was starting all over again.

We walked a few more blocks down Fifth Avenue and without any apparent reason, Daisy stopped abruptly. When I asked her why she stopped in front of that huge construction site, Daisy told me that it was the famous Ground Zero which was known across the globe for having been the sight of the World Trade Center, where the twin towers used to be. Then on September 11th, 2001 a cowardly terrorist act brought the towers down. On this day thousands of innocent lives were lost or affected and within a few hours millions of people lost hope and for some time, they even lost faith in God.

But even facing a cowardly act of this size, not only the Americans, but many people around the world, independent of their race, religious beliefs or color came together and re-conquered their hopes and their faith in God with the hopes of rebuilding their lives and strengthening the democracy. This is why Daisy asked me that we should close our eyes for a minute, out of respect for all those involved in that episode. After a minute, Daisy and I opened our eyes, wiped away our tears and started back on our journey.

Well, after walking a little more, we saw a bunch of kids playing in a small park and I went crazy when I saw some of them playing with a ball, we were dogs after all. I tried to play with them, but Daisy pulled me by the tail and chewed me out saying that we had an important task to carry on and that unfortunately there was no time for fun and games. I also knew that our task was very important and after what just happened I gave up on the idea of playing with them and most of all, with that marvelous little ball.

It was already after lunch time when I told Daisy I was starving. She was very hungry too, so we stopped near a little sandwich cart. We did a few tricks and luckily the girl who was selling the sandwiches fell in love with us and gave us two hotdogs. So we quickly ate them up and were on our way, without even thanking the adorable young girl. The hotdogs were really delicious. Daisy and I ate quickly and without losing a moment's time we continued on our big journey.

We had already walked for dozens of miles and my paws had blisters on them, I think Daisy's did too. So I asked her if it would be long before we arrived, but before she could answer me, I fell into a small hole where the sewer workers were doing a job. Luckily the hole wasn't too deep and I didn't get hurt. I think that Daisy wished she didn't have a nose when she helped me get out, because the stench was pretty bad. Luckily nearby there was a car wash, you know the kind where the cars go in dirty and come out the other side perfectly clean.

Well, at this point in the story you already know Daisy pretty well, so it's easy to guess what she wanted me to do next. Yeah, that's right, she asked me to go through the car wash where the cars were washed, so that I could take a bath. I agreed readily since the stench was horrible and I would have a chance to cool off. The bath was delightful and even my dear owner's old hat smelled nicely. So, again I could get right next to her.

I asked her again if we were close to our destination and at this time I was careful not to fall into another hole. Finally she told me that we were close, so close that the neighborhood dogs had all started wagging their tails and barking at her. I will confess that I became a little jealous, but after a few minutes my jealousy feelings went away when Daisy showed me the mansion that was also my dear owner's home. We walked just a few more feet and we arrived and the main entrance of the mansion. We had a sense of accomplishment and we were overcome with happiness. Now more than ever we knew that we would be able to save Mr. Robert's life.

Chapter 13

We were already in front of the main gate of Mr. Robert's mansion. We knew we were just a couple hundred feet away from the main entrance of that beautiful white house that looked more like a castle, surrounded by numerous gardens with roses, daisies and tulips among other magnificent types of flowers. The problem was we didn't know how to get in especially because the gate was close. So, the only option was to ring the bell. We made several attempts, but they were unsuccessful, since the button to ring the bell was up high. We were tired so we decided to wait until someone showed up around there and would see us.

We waited in front of that gate for a long time, we even lost track of time. It was started to get dark when we heard a loud noise and then the sky got very bright as if we were in the middle of spring. I knew that shortly after we would be drenched, forced to take another bath. Within a few seconds it started to rain and I think out of instinct we went to the gate and started to bark like crazy. Normally with that much noise we would have gotten the attention of someone in the neighborhood, but because of the distance between one mansion and the other and the deafening noise of the rain and thunder it was nearly impossible.

We were already totally soaked when a vehicle came in our direction. It was raining a lot, so much so that even Daisy couldn't see much of anything. However this vehicle turned on a bunch of lights, parked very close to the main gate and then we were finally able to see that it was a state police car that had been patrolling that area. A few seconds after the vehicle stopped, the police officer got out of the car, came in our direction, kneeled down and very attentively asked us if we were lost. With the help of a flashlight, he looked at the little collar that Daisy used, which had her registration number, name and address. While the officer was checking the information on Daisy's collar, I had the opportunity to see his face close up. After looking at him carefully, I was certain that I knew that policeman from somewhere. As hard as I tried, I couldn't remember where or when I had seen him. After he was done checking the information on the collar, the police officer got up, smiled and in a very loving manner told us that most likely the kids had forgotten us outside. Daisy tried to tell him that there were no kids in that house, but I was pretty sure that the police officer didn't understand a thing, after all, Daisy was only barking...

The policeman was very big and after he got up, he rang the bell which in reality was an intercom. He very quickly informed the people that lived there about us being there and within seconds Daisy and I saw that several lights in the garden had been turned on. Shortly after, the main entrance door opened. It was already night time and due to the distance and the heavy rain, Daisy and the officer could only see that two people were coming over in our direction, but it was impossible to distinguish who they were. A few more lights when on automatically as these people got closer to the gate. That's when Daisy was able to identify them and she told me that it was Mrs. Thelma and the governess at the mansion.

Right after Mrs. Thelma and the governess got to the gate; the police officer introduced himself and told them that the two dogs belonging to this address had been forgotten outside. Mrs. Thelma told the officer that they hadn't forgotten them outside, but rather that Daisy ran away when they were at a pet shop in Manhattan and that I didn't belong to her, that most likely I belonged to another family nearby. The police officer and Mrs. Thelma bent down again to see if I was wearing anything to identify who I was while the governess was trying in vain to hold Daisy back.

As he kneeled down, the policeman again lit up my face with the flashlight. Immediately Mrs. Thelma started crying happily when she saw that her father's hat was on my head. As a manner of thanking me, Mrs. Thelma started kissing me as she removed the old hat from my head. The police officer had no idea what was going on, until Mrs. Thelma stopped crying. She explained to him that her father, Mr. Robert, had Alzheimer's and that he had gone missing a while ago. She also told the officer that one morning the governess had gone out for a walk with Mr. Robert and that she came back without him. Somehow her father had gotten lost and since that time no one had any information about him or his whereabouts.

The police officer was surprised, but also very moved by the story he had just heard. He called the governess over to them so that he could share the good news with her. The governess came over to where we were standing as the police officer had asked, but when she saw the hat she started to shake and cry a lot. The officer and Mrs. Thelma were surprised by the unexpected reaction of the governess. That police officer was very experienced and he quickly asked Mrs. Thelma for permission to continue the conversation inside the house. Mrs. Thelma noticed that the police officer suspected that something was going on, so she allowed him to come inside.

However, before we went in, the policeman asked Mrs. Thelma if his partner could also go inside with us, since the entire time he had remained inside the vehicle. Daisy and I thought that it was odd that the other officer had stayed inside the car that whole time, but when the officer opened the door for his partner, I was totally surprised. It wasn't just any K-9 it was my best friend, who also recognized me as soon as he saw me. As soon as I saw Jimmy, I remembered how it was that I knew that officer; he was my dear friend's partner from the time that I participated in the K-9 training.

So, all of us went inside the house, but none of us really knew what was going to happen. After we were inside, the police officer closed the door, took a few steps toward the middle of the living room and finally, in a very polite manner, started asking the governess some questions. Seeing that she was quite nervous and shaking the whole time, the officer started to make his questions more direct and focused on Mr. Robert's disappearance, but now with a more serious, threatening tone. It didn't take long before the governess started to cry a lot and say that she regretted what she had done. Mrs. Thelma was quite upset and also crying, asked what had happened and finally the governess told her the whole truth in front of the police officer.

According to the governess, Mrs. Thelma's husband had given her a lot of money to take Mr. Robert out and leave him somewhere in Manhattan, so that the poor guy would get lost and not be able to come back home. Also, according to the governess, Mrs. Thelma's husband threatened her as well because she was in the US illegally.

After the governess' confession, the police ordered her arrested and while she was being handcuffed, a man's voice asked what was going on; it was Mrs. Thelma's husband. As soon as the police officer saw him also ordered him arrested, but Mrs. Thelma's husband tried to escape, a cowardly act, running toward the garden while the police officer was still busy trying to handcuff the governess. The policeman ordered his partner to get him, but for the first time ever, Jimmy disobeyed an order. To my surprise, Jimmy told me that I knew what to do and that this was my chance to prove my abilities.

I had already been trained to be a K-9 and I couldn't disappoint my friend. So, in act of bravery, I ran to the garden and even in the dark I quickly captured Mrs. Thelma's husband. After Jimmy and his partner arrived, he was finally handcuffed and taken to the police cruiser. After a few minutes a police van arrived at the house and took the criminals to the police station. Hopefully they will be locked up for many years.

After the criminals had been taken away and she had calmed down some, Mrs. Thelma spoke to the officer and it was decided that we would to go Manhattan that same evening to look for Mr. Robert. Since there wasn't enough space for all of us in the police cruiser, Mrs. Thelma asked her driver to prepare the limousine. While we waited one of the employees fed Daisy and I, Jimmy didn't want anything to eat because, according to him, it was against police regulations. While we ate, Jimmy praised me for my performance in capturing Mrs. Thelma's husband. According to Jimmy I had made him, and everyone, very proud.

Daisy and I had barely finished eating when Mrs. Thelma called us. Finally it was time to go looking for my master and it was decided that Daisy and I would ride in the limousine with Mrs. Thelma. The police car was following us, since Daisy and I were the only ones who knew where our dear owner was. The way back was faster this time and as soon as we entered Manhattan Daisy and I started barking, trying hard to give guide to the limousine driver on the right path. But it wasn't working, so finally Mrs. Thelma asked the driver to stop and open the door, so that Daisy and I could run free and guide them to the right spot. We were followed closely at all times by the limousine and the police cruiser. Soon we spotted the location where Mr. Robert should have been.

Happy and proud, Daisy and I ran over to the old marquee to find our dear owner and the two vehicles stopped. Immediately, Mrs. Thelma, the police officer and Jimmy came over to the location, but Mr. Robert wasn't there. We felt totally hopeless; Daisy and I didn't know what to do. Jimmy was trained for emergency situations, so right away he found a small wallet in one of the corners of the marquee and immediately brought it to Mrs. Thelma. When she saw the little wallet, Mrs. Thelma started to cry, since she was certain it belonged to her father. When she opened the wallet and saw a photo of her kissing her dear father, there was no doubt it was his.

We all became very emotional upon finding the wallet, even the police officer, which although he was very experienced, couldn't hold back his emotions and cried as well. Immediately, a mixture of love, tenderness, longing and concern took place of the environment and for a moment we all stood there in silence. I felt completely useless, since even though I had done everything that was in my power, I wasn't able to help them and all had been in vain.

Finally, Daisy broke the silence with a lot barking and I remembered that I had placed a GPS in the sole of Mr. Robert's shoe. Jimmy was very surprised by this and asked me how I had done that. So I explained to him how I had removed that GPS that was just under my skin and once again Jimmy praised me and also told me that I could be the best K-9 of all time, but that for him it was enough that I was his best friend.

In a way that only police officers understand, Jimmy tried to get his partner's attention. His partner at that moment was trying unsuccessfully to comfort Mrs. Thelma. Jimmy was barking a lot which got the police officer to come over to us. Immediately Jimmy showed him the small scar on my front paw. It was still visible, since the fur hadn't grown over it fully. The officer didn't understand what Jimmy was telling him with that gesture. So, we ran over to the police car and the policeman knew then that Jimmy and I wanted to tell him something, so he followed us.

Jimmy knew that all K-9s were monitored by GPS's, so when we go to the police car, he simply pointed at the computer screen with his paw and finally his partner realized that almost all of the signals that were emitted by the GPS's were all pointing to one location, the K-9 training center, with the exception of two signals that were showing two completely different locations. When he checked the computer in his cruiser, he identified both locations. The first one was Jimmy's GPS that flashed very quickly, because of its close proximity. But the other signal was flashing slowly, which clearly showed that it was far away, probably miles from there. For me, the location of the second GPS told me that my efforts hadn't been in vain.

When he checked his computer for the full address for the signals coming from the second GPS, the police offer cried out happily, since the address was for a public homeless shelter. Immediately Mrs. Thelma, Daisy and the limousine driver ran over to us. The police officer gave them all the good news; finally we knew where Mr. Robert was. In the midst of tears and laughter, we all got back into our cars again and now we all had one destination, a destination that would take us to our dear master.

Everyone got in their cars quickly; obviously we were all very anxious to rejoin our lovable owner. Finally the cars started moving, but soon after, the police car stopped and the police officer signaled for us to stop as well. He got out of his car and came over to our vehicle. Mrs. Thelma opened the limousine window right away. She wanted to know what was happening. The police officer told her that he had a flat tire. Right away she asked her driver to help the dear officer change the tire, but he refused the offer and asked if he and Jimmy could continue on the quest with us. Mrs. Thelma asked him if was against police regulations for an officer to abandon his vehicle. The officer answered yes, that he could even be fired for this, but he didn't want to miss that meeting for anything in the world. So, with a beautiful smile, Mrs. Thelma invited him to come into the limousine and we finally went on our way.

Within a few minutes we arrived at the homeless shelter. We all got out of the limousine quickly and ran to the front door. Since it was late, the door was closed, but because we had the police officer with us, they allowed us to go in. We were received by a very friendly woman which worked there as a volunteer. After Mrs. Thelma and the police officer explained why we were there, the woman let us all in.

Within a few seconds we all were able to see Mr. Robert and we ran over toward him. We really missed him terribly and we were very anxious to see him. However, as we got closer we saw a woman and her daughter speaking with Mr. Robert very politely while they were putting a bandage on his elbow. Mrs. Thelma was moved by seeing this woman and her daughter paying so much attention to her father, especially because they didn't work there, they were simply two homeless people.

As we got closer, Mrs. Thelma kneeled down in from of her father and with her eyes filled with tears asked the woman her name and what she was doing there. The woman told Mrs. Thelma that her name was Judy and her daughter's name was Grace. She went on to say that they had lived in the shelter for a while because she couldn't get a job. Still in tears, Mrs. Thelma instantly offered her a job as her governess and also invited both of them to come live with her in the mansion. She then asked the driver to take them to the limousine.

I was overcome with emotion, especially because I recognized Mrs. Judy's voice, her and her daughter Grace were the same ones that had given me food and played with me under that overpass the day of the big snowstorm last winter. Thanks to Mrs. Thelma, they now had a home. In reality, out of all the people in that shelter, I think that Mrs. Judy and her daughter were the exception and not the rule. What I mean is that most of the people who were there had simply lost their hope and faith in God.

Mrs. Thelma knew that her father needed urgent medical care so very quietly she asked the police officer to call an ambulance. While we waited, Mrs. Thelma let Daisy and I show our affection to our dear master, who in return also showed his affection to us. The ambulance arrived within a few minutes and the paramedics quickly took care of Mr. Robert. Mrs. Thelma asked the limo driver to take all of us home. She thanked the police officer and Jimmy, kissed them both and then got into the ambulance with her father.

Chapter 14

While the chauffeur took us over to the limousine, Daisy and I thanked Jimmy for everything he had done and we said our goodbyes. The chauffeur opened the door so that Daisy and I could get in. While Mrs. Judy and Grace waited for us, the chauffeur let the ambulance leave first and then he drove us to a fast food restaurant since all of us were very hungry, but above all everyone was happy. The chauffeur, Mrs. Judy and Grace stayed at the restaurant for over an hour. Unfortunately Daisy and I couldn't go in, but Grace within a few minutes brought us several sandwiches. Daisy and I turned into big blobs of fur from eating so much. After a while they all left the restaurant and we were on our way home.

As soon as we arrived, Mrs. Judy was now officially the new governess. She asked for help from one of the other employees at the mansion and soon little Grace was nicely settled in her new room and ready to go to sleep. Later, very lovingly, Mrs. Judy fixed up a bed for me right next to Daisy's old bed, served us a bowl of fresh water and we all went to bed. Daisy and I were still very awake and energized after everything that had happened. But we were also worried about Mr. Robert's health; after all we still didn't know the true state of his health. After talking for a little while, we started to feel sleepy and we both went to sleep.

The next day Daisy and I woke up very early, ate breakfast and went outside to the gardens to play. It was a Saturday and it was a really wonderful, sunny day. Grace was already in the garden playing on the swing, but when she saw Daisy and me, immediately stopped, got off the swing and ran over to greet us. The three of us played for several hours. Every so often I had an anxious feeling in my heart; after all we still didn't have any news about our master. Luckily the feeling subsided every time I heard Grace's laughter.

After a few hours, Mrs. Judy called us over and told everyone that Mr. Robert was doing well and that probably he and Mrs. Thelma would come home the next day. We were all very happy about this news and to celebrate Mrs. Judy served everyone ice cream. Actually, this was the first time I had ever tried ice cream. Later Mrs. Judy called for the chauffeur and we all went to Manhattan, this time just to go to the pet shop. We arrived in a few minutes and several people attended to our needs. Within a few hours, Daisy and I were groomed, had an amazing bath and also received new clothes and toys...all this and even ice cream for dogs!

Grace had a great time with all of that like me; I think she never had so much fun. Her mother had also told her that the next stop was going to be a specialty shop, just for girls. Certainly she too would get a lot of presents! In the end we all got new clothes and toys. We returned to the mansion, everyone was very tired and very hungry. Luckily the staff at the mansion served us dinner right away and I no longer had to eat Italian food all the time. Everyone here at the mansion respected Daisy and me a great deal so each of us had our own type of dog food that we preferred. After dinner we went to sleep since we all knew that the next day was going to be a very special one.

Despite the anxiety, we slept well all night, the morning sun already invaded and light up every corner of my new home Daisy and I were barely awake and Grace was already waiting there for us to play. Finally it was Sunday and we were all very excited since we would see our dear owners again. All of us ate and then quickly went out to play. The day was truly very special, even though Mrs. Thelma was at the hospital, she had asked the chauffeur to go out and buy a real playground for Grace with a swing, a slide and more!

We played outside for several hours, but with each passing hour I felt more and more anxious about seeing my dear owner. Luckily the driveway gate opened and it was the limousine bringing home our beloved owner and Mrs. Thelma. All of the staff at the mansion as well as Grace, Daisy and me ran to meet the limousine to welcome them home. Mrs. Thelma opened the door right away and with the help of the chauffeur, got our owner out of the car. Mr. Robert looked totally different, I almost didn't recognize him. In just two days he had put on weight and instead of his old and dirty clothes he was well kept and clean and had all the comforts he deserved.

After helping my dear owner out of the car, they took a wheelchair out of the trunk. At first I felt apprehensive; after all he never needed to use a wheelchair before. But then I heard Mrs. Thelma telling Mrs. Judy that the wheelchair was needed so that her father could avoid getting hurt again. Mrs. Judy understood why Mrs. Thelma was worried, after all when we found Mr. Robert he was being treated by Mrs. Judy precisely because he had fallen and injured his elbow. Well, after everyone was out of the limousine, we all went inside the house and were very happy that Mr. Robert was back at home. I was so happy about my dear owner being back at home that I bumped into a small statue that broke when it hit the floor. Everyone was taken by surprise by the noise, including my owner.

Without any delay, Mrs. Thelma ran over to me and very carefully got me out of there. Mrs. Judy also came over to help and told Mrs. Thelma that I probably had Cataracts since she had seen me bump into several objects aside from the fact that my eyes' pupils were always whitish. Mrs. Thelma patted me on the back and said that the following day she would take me to see the veterinarian. In spite of this incident, things were as usual that day and soon after we went to sleep.

The next morning, just like Mrs. Thelma had said I was taken to a specialist for an eye examination. I already had that same exam before so I was pretty calm about everything. However, when the doctor told Mrs. Thelma that the problem was Hereditary

Cataracts and that they could operate immediately, the story changed. I was full of fear, but was hopeful that maybe Mrs. Thelma would refuse to pay for the surgical procedure. But I was wrong...she immediately authorized the procedure and within a few minutes I was getting prepared for the surgery!

I didn't even really have time to feel scared because they quickly gave me the anesthesia and I was out. I wasn't sure how long I was there but when I woke up I was already in another room and Mrs. Thelma was smoothing down my eyebrows with her fingers just like Mr. Joseph used to do so many years ago. I could never forget that loving gesture. Finally, a few hours later even though I was still a little dizzy from the anesthesia we went back to the mansion where everyone was waiting for me, just like they did when my dear owner returned home. I was feeling like a king, everyone doting on me, bringing me toys and ice cream. I felt like they were doing more for me than I really deserved...

For a few days I was totally blind since they made me use a kind of bandage that covered up both of my eyes. I had no idea if the surgery had been a success or not. I didn't even know if I would be able to see again, but one find morning one of the nurses from the clinic came to the house at the request of Mrs. Thelma and within a few minutes removed the bandages that covering my eyes. I immediately started to cry out of happiness, because for the first time in my life I could see everything clearly. Everything looked even more beautiful than before, but sadly my dear owner wasn't there to share this happy moment with me.

I was totally euphoric and after licking Mrs. Thelma's face and the nurse's face, I ran to the yard where Grace and Daisy were playing. Daisy was very moved when she saw that I was able to see perfectly and I was even more in love with her when I was able to see her beautiful face clearly. But there was still someone very important left that I wanted to see with clarity, my dear owner. Unfortunately I had to wait a few more hours since the chauffeur took him to a specialized center, one that helps people with Alzheimer's disease. Well, I had to try to understand especially since this place was very good for him. Aside from the medical specialists he also had the companionship of many friends, people like him, who also had Alzheimer's.

I would really like to think that perhaps my dear owner's disease had a cure much like there was a cure for the problem with my eyes. But sadly as we all know no one has found a definitive cure for this disease. Maybe if big companies and the government invested more in research it would be possible. The problem is that many don't care about it, simply because it is somewhat of an invisible disease and things that are invisible don't really bother anyone at all.

A few more hours went by until finally the chauffeur brought Mr. Robert home. I ran over to the limousine and I anxiously waited for the chauffeur to help him out of the car. It wasn't long before I could finally see my dear owner's handsome face. That day, I spent the entire rest of the day with him, right by his side.

Mrs. Thelma was being very good to all of us, Mr. Robert was receiving the best treatment that money could buy, Mrs. Judy was a totally changed woman, full of pride, her daughter Grace was finally having a happy childhood, Daisy was always being spoiled and pampered and me, well I could finally see the world with sharpness and clarity, as it really was, without any of the shadows that had followed me throughout my entire life! I felt that all of us should show our gratitude to Mrs. Thelma, since one way or another she was the one who had changed everybody lives.

Since she was admired by all, Daisy and I thought that Mrs. Thelma was a happy person. One day when we overheard a conversation between Mrs. Judy and the chauffeur we discovered that deep down inside Mrs. Thelma was very sad. She always wanted to have children, but God hadn't blessed her that gift. After we found this out Daisy and I finally were able to understand why Mrs. Thelma always bought so many toys for Grace.

We really wanted to see Mrs. Thelma totally happy and fulfilled, so we started to pray every night that this would happen. Daisy and I somehow knew that this would be possible if we had total faith in this desire. So, for a long time we believed in this and we never gave up. A few months went by and Mr. Robert was doing much better, he was already much stronger, very different from the poor old guy that I met under that little bridge in Central Park. But, Mrs. Thelma still hadn't fulfilled her biggest dream.

One Sunday morning while we were having breakfast outside by the pool, Mrs. Thelma received a phone call and she went totally pale. Right away she called the chauffeur and they left a few minutes later. We were all very worried, including Mrs. Judy, since she had no idea what was going on. A few hours passed until she returned. The gates at the end of the driveway opened and then the limousine parked right in front of the main entrance.

The chauffeur got out and opened the door for Mrs. Thelma, who was all smiles. She got out of the car and then waited for someone else to get out…in a few seconds, to our surprise, a girl got out of the car. Daisy and I ran over and started licking the girl who kneeled down and hugged us. It was little Bruna, Mr. Francesco's daughter. She was now two years older, but she was the same girl, loving and obedient, always protecting all of her pets. She had waited a long time to have a new family that truly loved her.

Finally God had blessed Mrs. Thelma with the arrival of little Bruna and now we all knew that Mrs. Thelma was a totally happy and fulfilled woman! Our house seemed like paradise. My dear owner got better with each passing day, Mrs. Thelma was always singing; Bruna, Grace, Daisy and I were always playing in the yard. It was almost too good to be true. Our lives were perfect. The kids even planned a wedding ceremony for Daisy and me…can you

121

imagine? With a cake and everything that Mrs. Thelma ordered for the occasion. Well, after the ceremony and eating lots of cake and ice cream, Daisy and I went outside to play with the kids.

A few more months went by and we were all still doing well and happy. My dear owner continued to go the specialized center three times a week to get treated for Alzheimer's. As a way of showing her gratitude for the hard work of the entire medical team at the center, Mrs. Thelma organized a special trip to Long Island. Surely it would be a great opportunity to socialize and for the patients to have direct contact with nature. They could feel the sand between their toes, hear the sounds of the ocean and smell that special scent of the sea.

We were all invited to be a part of this wonderful outing, including the kids and the pets. We were all very excited about this event, especially Daisy and I since we would have the chance to play with all of the patients and show how much we love them. The majority of the patients are elderly and for one reason or another, for heartless reasons, they didn't receive visitors, much less any love or attention from their families. So, we were all waiting impatiently for the big day which was fast approaching.

Finally the long awaited day came. We woke up and although it was very earlier, the rays of sunshine were already shining in through the mansion windows and we were sure that this Sunday was going to be special. Mrs. Judy, with the help of one of the staff, served breakfast for everyone, but Daisy wasn't feeling well and didn't eat a thing. She was most likely so anxious that she couldn't eat. So we all rushed and ran to the yard where the chauffeur was already waiting for us. The limousine was quite big so quickly we were all inside and ready to go. We lived relatively close to Long Island so it didn't take long for us to smell the scent of the salty air. In a few minutes we arrived at the beach we had chosen to visit. Everyone was there waiting for us. As soon as we got out of the limousine, Bruna, Grace and I ran to the edge of the ocean. Daisy didn't follow, but rather laid down in the sand, most likely because she wanted to soak up some sun. I didn't really think much of it, since after all, we all know how women are and Daisy wasn't different. I played with Bruna and Grace for a while at the edge of the water, but then I decided it was time to give some love and attention to the others, not just Mr. Robert, but everyone. So, I called to Daisy to help me since there were a lot of older folks there with Alzheimer's and they all deserved our love and attention.

With some difficulty, Daisy got up and finally we walked over to where our dear owner was in the company of a group of very animated elders. When we got over there Daisy and I started playing with everyone and entertaining them with our tricks. All of a sudden, Daisy lay down in the sand again, but this time moaning and groaning quite a bit. Almost all of the old folks bent down immediately to try to help her with the exception of Mr. Robert which was on the wheelchair and a woman who within seconds took me away from there.

I was confused about what was going on and very worried about Daisy. I barked for a while to see if someone would let me get closer to her, but I finally gave up and lay down in the sand. A few minutes passed and the big group that had formed around Daisy thinned out and finally I could see her tail moving. Immediately I got up and run over to her. This time, no one stopped me. As soon as I got over to the love of my life I was able to see that she had given birth to many little baby puppies. I was so close to my true love and my beautiful children, just a few feet separated me from my family…but my legs went weak and I started to cry out of emotion. Everyone that had helped Daisy stayed right there close to her side and they were also extremely moved by what they had just witnessed.

A few minutes went by and I regained my strength. I ran over to kiss Daisy and each of our baby puppies as all of the old folks that had helped with the birth process stood watch. I thanked my wife for giving me the most beautiful children a dog could have.

I was very moved by all this and now that my vision was perfect, even at a distance I could see my dear owner, my dear master, the man who made all of this possible, our lovable Mr. Robert, which even on his wheelchair and suffering from Alzheimer's had a very pleased and proud smile on his face!

For all these reasons, I wasn't able to hold back...I gently carried one of my beautiful puppy over to my dear owner, placing on his lap a part of me; placing in his lap my own son. With his eyes filled with tears and his wrinkled hands, my dear Mr. Robert patted my son gently and thanked me for our wonderful story.

I hope you have enjoyed this story. As you can see, I am very young to have lived through all of this. In reality this was the story of love and devotion between my father and his dear, beloved owner. Sadly they are no longer here with us, but they will always be remembered every time when you see a mistreated animal, an abandoned elderly, forgotten by his family, or perhaps if you are truly lucky, you will see them when you look up at the stars.

Please remember to always intensely love your elderly and pets, because they won't last forever.

The End